A MATTER OF TIME

I0589864

ED DAVIS

For Bruce

CONTENTS

FOREWORD

FRIDAY MORNING NOVEMBER 29, 2002 at 5 a.m. I sat down at my computer intending to write a full-length novel — 50,000 words in 24 hours. Setting aside the *why* and the *what* of the thing, the how is worth considering: 2,083 words per hour or 34.7 words a minute. What would that actually look like? Try this. *I'd have about five times as long to create this sentence as it has taken you to read it.* Could I physically do that?

Thanks to sophomore typing — perhaps the most valuable class I ever took — the mechanics were no problem. I can type sixty words a minute without breaking a sweat. But could I compose at 35 words a minute for 24 hours straight, and have it make any sense? A couple of test runs — a half-hour, then a full hour — produced mixed results. I could create coherent sentences, even string them together well enough. Telling an actual story was something else entirely.

It became abundantly clear that without a simple but detailed outline, I didn't stand a chance.

What resulted, as you can see in this short time lapse video, was a flip-chart: one page per chapter, one chapter per hour. It was a guide and a task master that kept me and the plot rushing forward in my attempt to keep up with the clock.

That's the *how*.

The *why* is little more complicated. Part of it was the sheer challenge. The *Write a Novel in a Month* phenomenon had just begun — a great concept that has inspired thousands of people to write novels and has produced some very good work. I wanted to see if I could do it in a day. Crazy, but there it is. This was a year after the twin towers came down. Things were changing so quickly in our country that it was sometimes hard to recognize it — or my place in it. I was looking for a way to grapple with both. Something to address the extraordinary times. For a writer, an explosion of words to push back against the possible implosion of our way of life seemed perfect.

Most importantly, though, a good friend had died the year before, died too young. In some fundamental way that I still don't fully understand, taking on this unlikely task was an opportunity for me to honor his memory.

As to the *what* — the story you are about to read — it is a cautionary tale of a time in the not-too-distant future when our country has traded away freedom for security. A leader who values control over the Constitution, who will go to any length to silence his enemies, and who has such sway over the media that it has become little more than his own private megaphone, has been elected. This man, and those around him, hang on to power at any cost.

Sound familiar?

I could not have known, when I wrote this sixteen years ago, how prescient parts of it would turn out to be.

The hero is condemned to die. This is the story of his last 24 hours, told one chapter per hour, and written in real time, one chapter per hour.

Did I reach my 50,000-word goal? No I did not. At just under 30,000 words, this is a novella, not a novel. About three hours into the effort, it became obvious that while I could type fast enough, I couldn't think fast enough. Did I capture some of the uncertainty of the times? I hope so. And I hope this story serves as a reminder to all of us — no matter how bad we think things are, if we aren't ever vigilant they can always get worse.

Did I write a story my friend Bruce would have appreciated? I think so, and this book is dedicated to him.

Jack London Lodge
Glen Ellen, Ca – August 23, 2018

CHAPTER ONE — NOVEMBER 28, 2010
TWENTY-FOUR HOURS LEFT

I'VE BEEN WATCHING the clock come up to 5 a.m. Not sleeping, and not surprised really. How could I sleep on this last night? It has been so quiet. I read someplace that on the night before an execution, Death Row is the quietest place on earth.

My name is Ed Davis. In just under twenty-four hours, I will be leaving this cell for the last time.

It's lonely, but I'm not alone — never alone. Guards are my constant companions, though they sit just outside my cell. Mr. Critchett is on duty now. We call each other "Mr." here. I am Mr. Davis. Very formal, very proper. Just one of many prison reforms from the past few years, this one more benign than most.

Critchett is hard to read. I'm not officially supposed to talk with the guards, nothing beyond the bare minimum required to go through the daily routine. But it is impossible not to. And it is impossible not to know them just from watching them. Mr. Critchett looks like a military man. When he stands, which is often, he stands erect, alert. The posture of a soldier at attention. He speaks carefully, as if giving and responding to orders. Like a pilot to his tail gunner maybe. I'm guessing that he likes his job, takes it seriously. I'm guessing that he is looking forward to tomorrow morning.

I know what will happen. I'm not supposed to, but I do. Some of the guards talk a bit more than others. Some of them like talking.

In just under twenty-four hours my cell door will open. Warden Yeager will be here. And Pastor Stedman and a couple of guards I won't know. The manacles will go on my ankles and wrists. I don't know why — but what is it that therapists say? The "why" questions will make you crazy. It's not like I could escape. San Quentin is more secure than ever; thanks to the recent changes, all our prisons are — *Better Prisons, Better Peace of Mind.* Who could argue with that?

We will step out the cell door and turn right. If we turned left we'd go a few yards down the hall to the cell block door, the one I entered through. Under the new system, once you walk in that door you almost never walk back out.

I will turn right. Shuffle down the hall a bit. Come to that other door. Go through it.

And I will step into the Rust Room.

I guess it used to be a green room back when they had the gas chamber, and later when they went to lethal injection. But now it's rust colored, kind of a reddish rust. The guard who shared that particular bit of information, Mr. Zebel, took particular delight in telling me that.

There will be no witnesses in the room, but the event will definitely be witnessed. Directly across the door from where I enter will be the GBS camera crew. The Government Broadcasting System carries most of the news events of the day — or at least those events that management thinks are worthy. They always cover executions. This particular broadcast, Mr. Zebel told me, will be brought to the public by the good people at Smith & Wesson. It seems appropriate.

Just to my left, standing at parade rest, will be a row of ten men and women. Each of them volunteers chosen from the Homeland Security Police, each of them specifically trained in the skills required for this particular task.

Each of them with a rifle at their side.

The guards will lead me to a spot marked on the floor and put a black mask over my head. There's a post behind the spot so they can strap me up, if necessary. Will it be necessary? Even this close to the time I don't know.

On the count the weapons will go up, the triggers will be pulled, and ten pieces of steel-jacketed lead will go crashing through my skull. None of this "one bullet and nine blanks" nonsense for them or for me.

I've been told that lethal injection was abolished not because it was ineffective but because it seemed timid, almost apologetic — as if the state didn't really want to perform this particular rite.

Some say the new method is actually kinder, quicker, almost instantaneous. Maybe. Mostly I think it looks better on TV. All but the one thing, that is. That's why the room is rust colored instead of green.

But that's forever from now, almost a whole twenty-four hours away. In the meantime, here I am in this cell where I've spent the last three months. A short time in retrospect but an eternity in its tedious unfolding.

And so little time is left.

So little.

I've got almost nothing in my cell, per the prison reforms. A six by ten room. Three concrete walls, and one nothing but bars with a small door in it. A cot, a desk, a chair, a toilet without a seat. Why no seat? It's not like I could hang myself with it. It's not like I'm not being watched twenty-four hours a day, both by the guards and cameras in my cell and in the hall.

No seat though.

No computer, no TV, no radio. There was a time when prisoners had those things. This new system is supposed to be more humane. By official thinking, it's like torture: giving a prisoner a glimpse of what's outside when they will never see it again. This way is more compassionate. And it leaves no doubt, as if the bars ever did, of who is in absolute control.

They do let me have some books, but only some. Anything by Mark Twain is fine, even Huck Finn, surprisingly. I'm guessing they've never read it. Nothing by Kurt Vonnegut. Hemingway and Jack London are on, Steinbeck and Fitzgerald off. Steven King is no problem — except for *Rita Hayworth* and *Shawshank Redemption* and *The Green Mile*.

As to visitors? Company? News? There's a new policy about those, too. Except for the guards, who rotate every eight hours, and a visit from Pastor Stedman once a week, I've been absolutely alone. Sure, I've got lawyers, a team of them working pretty much round the clock. But their work should have been done before I got here — or that's my current reasoning. Yes, they're still free to try to get me out. I'm just not free to help. It is supposed to be more compassionate this way, and the time goes more quickly they say.

Actually, I think they got that part right. The time does go quickly, Too quickly. And yet so slowly. I don't know how that can be, but it is — the months leading up to this day so short, the minutes so long.

None of us ever think much about time, at least not until we run out of it. We're only given so much — so many seconds in very minute — so many minutes in an hour — so many hours and days and weeks and months in our lives. We only get so much, and we almost never notice it, don't even think about it as it slips by, never to come again. A jail cell is a great place to think about time. To learn about it, come to understand — and hate — and crave — and fear it. Nobody knows time like a man who is almost out of it.

I'm almost out now. If I could, would I go back and reclaim some of the allotment that has already passed? Would I pull back those idle minutes spent doing what? Nothing. Less than nothing. Would I pick a time, a day, a place, a single event to relive? Or would I decide to put that time back in the bank so I could take it out and use it again, use it now? God yes! I would. I think I would. I know I wasted so much. So. Much. What I don't know is: what would I take back? What I don't know is: which of those minutes that seemed wasted led to others that weren't? Maybe led to others that were great — a lifetime that was great in so many ways. Yet — they all led finally to this night, this place, this cell.

I don't know what I'd take back or do over, but I do think about it.

I think about it all the time.

And why is it, right now, that the time seems to be racing by?

They put a clock on the wall out in the hall. I can hear it, see it, watch the second hand ticking, moving, speeding around the dial. I swear it's going faster now than last month, last week, yesterday — just a minute ago. I swear I can feel it speeding up. Maybe it is. Maybe I'm speeding up. Maybe it is getting too close, too real. I don't know what I thought this last day would be like. It's only just started, only less than an hour old, and already it isn't what I expected. I'm tired already. Lack of sleep for sure. But more than that, carrying this weight the past few months, knowing that the clock, whether moving fast or slow, was moving my way. And it wasn't going to stop.

I never thought it would speed up.

I never saw that coming.

Mr. Critchett just sits there watching me. Stoic, businesslike. I wonder if he has any idea at all what I'm thinking. I wonder if he has anything on his mind. Other than finishing his shift and heading home. Probably. Probably he's going through procedures in his head, last day procedures. What to do if I panic. What to do if I faint. Or cry. Or plead or beg? I'll try to make it easy on him — I don't see myself doing any of those things. But then — I didn't see myself here in the first place.

Damn that clock. I need to stop looking at it. The time is racing in here, sure, but what about time in the rest of the world? The rest of the world that I knew and know and love and will leave behind? It's still out there just beyond these walls. Sometimes if I close my eyes, I can feel it all there. Beyond reach. The cars, the offices, the boats on the bay. The activity that just goes on — around me, in spite of me. In spite of everything. I take some comfort in knowing that it's all still out there. But I can't let my mind go too far down that road. It's all still out there, but I'm not. I won't even be in here all that much longer.

I won't be at all.

No longer aware of San Francisco Bay and the city that lies beyond the row of high, barred windows in the wall opposite my cell door. They face southeast, I think. Sometimes the moon is visible, like now. A cradling moon I think they call it. A bright sliver, a crescent that cradles within it the shadow of the rest of the orb, like a child to its mother's breast. I think that means there will be good weather today. Good weather, like on the day that landed me here.

Almost six months ago on the city hall steps in my hometown of Elgin, California, I took a man's life. I wish I could say that it hadn't happened. I wish that more than anything, have wished it every long minute of every eternal day.

A spring afternoon, the kind people move to Elgin for, the kind they never leave because of. My friends and family there, and several hundred townspeople. And a lot of others and the GBS cameras.

I did in fact kill a man. A friend. In front of them all. According to the law of the land, I'm guilty as charged — guilty as hell.

And in just over twenty-three hours, they're going to kill me for it.

CHAPTER TWO
TWENTY-THREE HOURS LEFT

THIS IS ONE of the worst parts. Not the worst, maybe, but one of them. There is no privacy in prison, reformed or not, compassionate or not. No privacy. None. Maybe for security reasons like they say. Mostly I think it's because they don't ever want me to be in control. Of anything.

I've got to take a leak. At least I don't have to ask permission. But Mr. Critchett will need to watch. At least that is what he wants me to believe — that he *needs* to do it, all of it. It's procedure, it's orders, it's the way the system has to work. But why does he have to watch me pee? What possible harm can I do in that vulnerable moment?

I turn my back to him, which gives me what little pleasure there is to be had in this whole process. I try to put my mind somewhere else and let my body take care of itself.

It is all part of their plan to kill me, I get that. They want to do it in little pieces, fragments, little deaths, a bit at a time so that when the final act comes, the big bang, I'll be almost gone already. I think I've done pretty well at resisting the daily deaths. Largely because I can't make any sense of it, can't get my mind around the fact that these people — though they don't know me at all — actually intend to end my life.

I have also learned that there is a lot of me to kill and a lot of me they can never hope to reach. Will that be true even in the end? I wonder? I don't know about that part — I've never been very clear on how the *end of life* and *life after* stuff all works. But in spite of everything they've done — the small indignities and large — I still feel I'm pretty much who I am, who I was, who I wanted to be.

It's strange that there's one whole class of books they've never censored: books that have to do with spirituality. I guess they lump meditation in with everything else spiritual, so they've had no problem giving me books on Buddhist meditation, on healing, on the art of taking yourself within yourself. Of leaving by coming home. I practice the techniques — look at a wall, look out the window, look into that "middle space" and try to let my mind go. Some people recommend using the blackboard technique. See your mind as a blackboard full of the chalk words that are your life — everything that is you. Then slowly, very slowly, let your mind erase what's there. Turn the white lines and letters into blackness. Make the blackness bigger and bigger until the white lines are gone and the black is complete. Until you're truly open to think and feel what you will.

I try that method sometimes. It works as a start. But it somehow seems too easy. I know there is more. Which a few times, just a few, I've glimpsed. I think maybe I can get there. It's a place in the woods in summer. Evening after the sun has gone all the way down and the sky is dark. Stars are visible up through the trees, a canopy of stars through the green/gray canopy of fir and pine boughs. And ahead of me in the distance through the trees — lights. They twinkle as the evening breeze moves the branches. The breeze is fragrant with pine needles and musk and fern and the smell of a creek somewhere nearby. A warm breeze still carrying all the flavor of the day. As it moves the branches, lights in the distance seem to dance. I'm walking toward the lights, not yet close enough to see exactly where they are coming from, not quite close enough to hear the sound that comes with them. But there will be a sound, I'm sure of it. I think they are the lights of a pavilion, or maybe a lodge. I think it's warm and bright inside.

I know I want to be there.

I don't try to take my mind there too often. It has become too special for me — the feel of that place and the promise it holds. I get close, but only close. It's not that I'm afraid. I just don't think I'm ready.

The place I do go in my mind, whenever I can, is Elgin. It has been my home since 1975. "Where the wine country meets the redwoods," says the slogan on the welcome sign at the edge of town. About twenty miles from the Pacific Ocean, a dozen or so from the Russian

River, it is just a little town, a little spot on the map — mostly unnoticed for a hundred and fifty years. It was apple country in the beginning — gently rolling hills bathed in apple blossoms every spring, the smell of apples late summer and fall when the windfalls dotted the soft powdery earth of the orchards. The outlying hills hosted dairy farms and chickens and some truck gardens for the markets in town and the restaurants over in Santa Rosa. In the early days, it was just a place where people came for all the reasons that people go anywhere — and the people who came were of every stripe. Italian, Irish, Japanese. The Pomo and Miwok Indians were mostly gone by the time I arrived, but their bloodlines still hung on, and their names.

Everybody must feel that there is something special about the place they call home, or it wouldn't be home. I guess that's only right. But Elgin is special, going back long before I got there.

Maybe the land, or maybe the proximity to the ocean, maybe the people who washed up on its shore were different somehow. I don't know.

I do know the stories about the Wobblies who organized there back in the twenties. The Workers of the World found a willing ear in Elgin, not because there was much exploiting going on, just a lot of work. And in the Second World War, when the government rounded up all the Japanese in the West — many families from Elgin among them — those Italian and Irish and Greek farmers who remained behind formed a loose band of caretakers watching over the vacated farms. They kept them from going fallow and made sure that they were still there when the war was over.

Not all the history was pretty. As late as 1930 there was a lynching just one town over — and a big contingent from Elgin went to watch. People go astray sometimes.

It's always been a little town. Five thousand people give or take. Fire department's mostly volunteer. Just enough police officers to get the job done. A library, some schools, even our own *Elgin Tribune*. Ernie Joiner's the editor. I think a lot about Ernie. And I know he thinks about me.

The group of us that ended up there in the mid-seventies came for a hundred different reasons. Houses were cheap, San Francisco was just an hour south, the place felt right. The sixties brought communes to the hills toward the coast. Music up at the river most weekends, weather to die for. The kind of life a certain kind of person wanted. You didn't move to Elgin if you wanted what a city had to offer. You came for other reasons, good ones.

I don't have a clue how most adults make friends, but I know how we did: our kids. We were mostly young couples just a little past starting out, not nearly close to understanding where we were really going. But part of our journey was going to include kids, and we had 'em —two mostly. Some had two boys, others two girls. Jan and I had one of each; Noah was born in 1980, Emily four years later. When Noah started kindergarten at Dunbar School — was when our lives in Elgin really began.

A sense of community isn't something you can just create, just command, just order up — though some places clearly try. Ours just grew, and it grew around Dunbar School. It was not a one-room school by any stretch of the imagination, but it felt like that. Most of us worked full time, but we all figured out a way to be at that school. We did it for our kids, of course. But we also did it for ourselves.

We spent hours in the classroom, hours on the playground, hours volunteering for the Halloween Carnival, the Hoedown, the Talent Show. We helped put on Dunbar Days every spring —an absolute kid fantasy with nothing but games and food and families having fun — and a fire truck out on the playfield at the end to soak us all.

We lived at Dunbar.

And we met our neighbors.

And they quickly became our friends.

There were the Carrs — Cynthia and Gregg, with two boys, Jessie and Ben. The Panenchars — Chuck and Christina had two more boys, Lauren and Adrian. Anne and Bruce Kuschner were our best friends — we'd moved to town almost as a unit, and we helped raise Joel and Carmen just as they helped with Noah and Em. Ritch and Margie Foster had two boys, Deb and Rory Pool two girls. Mike Witkowski taught first grade at Dunbar, Sandi Everett taught kindergarten. Even if they hadn't wanted to be part of our group, they could not have avoided it — and their girls became like ours as well. Leigh and Maxine Hall had Amanda and Ben. Leigh was a family doctor in town; Maxine volunteered in the classrooms almost every day.

Without any of us knowing it or planning it, our family by affection grew and grew.

As the kids got older and the seventies turned into the eighties, our relationships started to grow beyond the school yard. We knew other people in town, sure, had other friends from elsewhere, made new friends as well. But the people we spent our time with, the people we missed when we went away, were those families from Dunbar that had become like our own.

I think a lot of friends drift apart as their kids do. The kids grow older, go to different schools, have different interests, and the parents grow distant.

We didn't. We liked what we had with each other, and we wanted more of it. We made our lives include theirs, because we cared. We loved them. Could not have imagined doing anything else.

Mostly my meditation goes to Elgin. So I mediate often in my cell. Sometimes I start with the blackboard, and sometimes — just sometimes – I try to glimpse the lights through the trees. But mostly I go to Elgin. I go there in my dreams, in my thoughts, in the moments when I'm tired and sick and afraid. I go there — and it is always there for me, just as my friends have always been there for me — just as I know they will be there for Jan and the kids when I'm gone. Everyone should have such a place — real if possible, imagined if not. Everyone should know that there is one place in all the world where they will never be turned away, never be hungry, never go without comfort when it's needed, never have to feel alone. Everyone needs such a place.

I need it now, every day.

So I meditate. I visit Elgin as often as I can. And, yes, I understand that if my journey, my life as an adult, had not started there, it would not be about to end here, just down the hall — twenty-two hours from now.

CHAPTER THREE
TWENTY-TWO HOURS LEFT

EVERY MORNING AT this time Mr. Critchett steps down the hall to my left, opens the door, and comes back pushing a cart with my breakfast — and his. I don't know if it's about efficiency or some sort of psychological game, but the guards eat what I eat. Or mostly they do, so the one element of control I have over them is the menu, at least on this, my last day. I suppose I should have ordered fried dog turds to test the system.

But instead I ordered the breakfast I always ordered when I was free. Link sausage, eggs over easy, hash browns, sourdough toast, a glass of orange juice, and Earl Gray tea. Not everybody likes Earl Gray, but it's my favorite. I can smell it on the cart now as he is rolling it up the aisle.

I've heard it said that you can almost never get a bad breakfast. God, am I testing that theory this morning. If there is anything to the notion that "atmosphere makes the meal," this should be the worst breakfast of my life. But it's as good as I remember.

I glance up at Critchett out in the hall there. Our eyes meet. He nods approval and keeps on eating. It is the closest thing to a personal moment that the two of us have had together in three months. I'll take it.

After breakfast, another daily routine. Another little indignity.

I get to leave my cell once a day. Our new federal prison system prizes personal hygiene, hygiene of all kinds, above almost everything else but security. And obedience. Once a day my cell door is opened and Mr. Critchett leads me down the hall to the left — toward the door that will take me out if I am ever to leave this place alive — and into the single, sanitary shower room on my block. We walk past two empty cells on the way there and on the way back. They've been empty since I arrived. I can't believe it's because they have no potential guests — the system has gotten more efficient in the last couple of years to be sure, and with that has come a significant rise in "check ins." Yet for whatever reason,

I'm the only guest in this wing of "Hotel Q." I've got it all to myself, me and my guards and nothing but time on my hands.

If only that were true.

Critchett has watched me take a leak, watched me throw up, watched me sit on my private little throne in my private little hell — or is it my own personal castle? Every man's home is one, they say. But all I've got is the throne.

As I undress for the shower and turn the water on, taking my time, Critchett averts his eyes. I don't get it — never will. Maybe it's some sort of odd respect. Maybe he's afraid of the intimacy. Maybe he likes it *too* much. But for these few minutes every morning, I can stand in this shower — where the warm water never runs out — and feel entirely alone. Naked and wet and alone. In my average day, this is about the best I can hope for. No, it could be better. If I could turn on the water and turn off the clock, I'd be perfectly content just to stand here under this showerhead and never come out.

But I can only stretch it so long — and though I know I'm not missing anything by lingering as long as

Critchett will let me, I always get out before he asks. It's a love/hate, good/bad thing for me. I love the shower, I hate the time it takes away. It makes me feel good for those few minutes, but then those minutes are gone from my rapidly dwindling supply, gone forever.

But today isn't going to be like every other day I've spent here, not even considering how it looks like it will end. Today I've got an actual schedule. Two copies came in on the breakfast cart, one for Critchett, one for me. Like an activities schedule at a resort hotel.

8AM. "Guard Change." God, am I not looking forward to that. Critchett, strange as he is, at least mostly leaves me alone. It would be a blessing if Zebel could do the same — but no blessings here. Just little deaths with every tick of the clock. Little deaths.

9AM. "Official Visit." No details, but I've got an idea already what it's going to be. Warden Yeager runs a tight ship. He's been in my cell many times. Never threatening, never intimidating, just doing his job — and he's going to be damned sure to do it right. Our visits have often brought surprises, frequently strange ones. The prison reforms have clearly been hard on prisoners, but I get the feeling they've been hard on guys like Yeager, too. I suspect he probably likes his job, or did once. I'm not so sure about now. But I do know that whatever the new manual says to do, he will do. Whether or not it makes any sense to him at all. A perfect bureaucrat, I suppose. How many of his type are out there now, in jobs big and small, important and trivial, all over the country? How many of them ever question what they are being asked to do, or if not actually question it, at least THINK about questioning it? Damn few, I think.

Damn few.

9:30 to Noon. "Light Schedule." No kidding, that's what it says. "Light Schedule." It sounds like a nice time to take a break between the morning shore visit to the shops and high tea in the master salon. Light fucking schedule. I'm smiling at that one, can't help but wonder if Yeager has even seen it. Some clerk somewhere must be having a laugh at our expense. Yes, this morning from 9:30 to noon Mr. Davis will be enjoying a light schedule. Taking a little rest before his midday meal. Composing himself in quiet thought, because in not too many hours, ten citizens stout and true are going to blast his brains all over the back wall of the Rust Room. A little light schedule is probably just what he needs.

Noon. "Lunch – Visit from Pastor Stedman." For lunch, I've ordered a turkey and cheddar sandwich on a Dutch crunch roll with everything, even onions. Usually I leave the onions off, but what the hell, today I'll go wild.

And a visit from Pastor Stedman. He's no more a pastor than I am the pope. Surely, they must all know that by now, yet they have still let him come in once a week, right from the start. His visits are all I've had, or almost all. How could the two of us have known when we were kids growing up together that it would one day come to this — a deli sandwich on death row.

2PM. "Official Visit – Warden Yeager." This one has me curious. I know they do a death watch on prisoners — but Jesus, haven't they got that covered. Cameras, Critchett, and Zebel after him. And what the hell am I going to kill myself with anyway — they haven't even given me a toilet seat.

I'm staring at this 2PM entry. There's something here, I'm sure of it. What the hell is Yeager up to? No, that's not right. What the hell are the powers that be up to? Yeager just runs the joint. They run him.

3PM. "Another Light Schedule."

I shit you not.

4PM. "Pastor Stedman" is scheduled to come in again. I know what this one is about. I don't want to think about it, but can't help myself. The outcome of the first of my two remaining appeals will be announced by then. You'd think the warden would want to tell me the results himself, but he never has. In fact, Yeager has never brought me ANY news about my case — nothing. It's all come from Stedman on his weekly visits. All the attempted strategies, all the appeals and pleas and legal gambits. Usually the news is days old by the time I get it. And always it's been the same.

Now only two appeals left.

Only two.

5PM. "Change of Guard." Zebel goes off shift, Cervantes comes on.

5PM to 7PM. You guessed it: "Light Schedule." Only this time they call it a light "Evening" schedule, which I guess somehow makes it different.

7PM. "Dinner." Man, am I looking forward to that. No really, I am. Meatloaf, mashed potatoes with brown gravy, string beans. And to drink — a cold beer. My first since I walked in this door, and I have the impression that granting the request was quite a big deal. But they did it — in the name of compassion, I suppose.

7PM to 10PM. "A Quiet Evening on the Cell Block."

Whoever the clerk was that put this thing together, he must have been running out of material by this time. At least he tried — I hope for my benefit. He wanted to give me one last smile on my way out. I hope so. I doubt it.

10PM. "Interview with the Press." That'll be Ernie Joiner. God love Ernie. I wonder how he swung it. I never thought I'd feel so close to anybody in the media, particularly not with what the media has become these days. But God love Ernie. Near the end, at least, I'll have a good conversation with a man I respect. At least I'll have that much.

11PM. "Pastor Stedman." That will be to report on the second appeal, I suppose. I don't have any idea how they can know this far in advance exactly when the word will come down. Maybe they just scheduled him here because it's the "eleventh hour," when such things are supposed to happen. At least I'll get to see him one more time — once more before the very last.

Pastor Stedman. I don't know how Steve has kept it up all these months, except that he's Steve, and he knows that this is the most he can do. No one ever calls him Steve anymore, or hardly anyone. Mostly we call him FA. Albert, Alberto, most properly Fat Albert. He loved Bill Cosby when we were kids and loved most of all the stories about buck-buck and the baddest buck-buck player of them all, Fat Albert. The name just stuck, and lots of other names over the years. Pastor Stedman is the name that none of us would have believed, though amazingly, the authorities have bought it these past three months. He is a pastor of sorts, or a minister more properly. In the Universal Life Church with a certificate to prove it. Over the years, he's done a lot of weddings — tentatively at first, but he had a natural aptitude for it.

He's read at funerals and helped a lot of people celebrate and survive both good times and bad. Tomorrow morning he'll add a new service to his list as he walks me out this cell door and down the hall to the right.

I try not to think about that walk, try in every way I can. But still I do. What will those steps feel like? What will I be thinking? Outside right now the sun is working its way up. I can see it through the high windows in the hall outside. But tomorrow morning it will be dark, all dark — the darkest I've ever known. I try not to think about it. Try to think of anything else.

I try.

Midnight to 5AM. The agenda is blank here. Our clerk either gave up or just couldn't figure out what to write. Midnight to 5AM. The long marches of the last long night. That seems like it will be forever from now. I know it will take forever — and I know that it won't.

The long marches of the night, indeed.

A night that, for me, will never end.

CHAPTER FOUR
TWENTY-ONE HOURS LEFT

I HEAR FOOTSTEPS in the hall, steps I've come to recognize well in my three months here. Mr. Zebel is coming on shift.

And there he is. The guards here don't salute, though I actually think Critchett would like to. It would suit him somehow. Zebel, on the other hand, would never salute. If forced to, he would find a way to do it that communicated exactly who is in charge.

They exchange a few words, and now it's Critchett's footsteps receding down the hall. Strange, but I thought he would at least say goodbye, say something. Strange.

"Good morning, Mr. Davis. How are we feeling this morning?" Nothing menacing in those words, nothing sinister. But the way he says them, has every morning, makes my skin crawl.

Usually I try not to look at Zebel, but this morning I do. It's his eyes that are hardest to look at. It's not that they're deformed — they don't "go funny" as the kids in school used to say. In fact, they're almost too perfect: blue, clear, cold — and something more. If I watch carefully it's as if I can almost see something moving behind his eyes — something I know I'd just as soon never encounter up close.

"Wouldn't pass the gut-check," my best friend Rich would say, if he was ever unlucky enough to meet the man. Rich and I went through high school together, and we've worked side by side most of our adult lives at the plastics company Rich owns. Lately I've mostly been running it — up until the last three months, that is. Through the years, we've figured out most of what there is to know about making plastic parts, making a decent place for people to work, and making a living. But one of the hardest lessons to learn was the gut-check. Somebody would apply for job, and the references would look great, the resume great. And the interview almost made to order. We'd listen, and we'd listen — each waiting for the other to pin down what was wrong.

Finally we named it — the gut check. It didn't matter how good somebody looked, if they didn't feel right they probably weren't. Zebel wouldn't have passed the gut-check by a mile.

And thinking of Zebel — of everything that can be wrong with a man — I can't help but think of the SOGs and of everything that can be right. From the very beginning, the SOGs had the gut-check aced. Always did, always will. I guess we're famous now, or maybe infamous because of me. But when we started out, we were just a bunch of guys that got to talking at a Valentine's Party.

It must have been around 1994, though I can't remember exactly. We were at one of those great parties that somebody in the Elgin posse threw a couple of times a year. There were movie parties, soup-group parties, any reason to get together. This was a Valentine's party. I'm sure of it, because I remember lots of red and white — on the walls and on the guests. The Halls were there, the Fosters, Kuschners, Witkowskis, Carrs and Pools — Rory and Deb on their motorcycle — Valentine bikers. Chuck & Christina Palenchar, Ron & Sandi Everett.

All our friends were there. All our younger kids were being watched by some of our older ones.

It was Rory who started it, I think. "Don't I see you running some evenings, out on Warm Springs Road?"

Yeah, that was me he saw. And sometimes he saw Leigh Hall in the early mornings in the Regional Park, sometimes Bruce with his dogs.

"Why don't we get together for a run some weekend? Maybe Sunday morning at my house? How about 8:00 o'clock?"

That was all it took.

Rory asked everybody that night. Leigh, Bruce, Mike, Chuck and I were in for sure. Greg Carr said he'd only run if somebody was chasing him. Ritch Foster said he'd think about it, but mostly he and running didn't get along so well, particularly the first half mile.

So it was six of us that Sunday. We started to run together.

And soon others joined us.

And we never stopped.

Mike was still teaching up at Dunbar then. He's retired now, of course, but then he was right in the thick of it — and when he wasn't telling awful jokes, he would tell us about school. Chuck was still working for the phone company, as he had been for over twenty years. An inquisitive mind and all those years in a truck meant that Chuck knew more about our town and our county than the rest of us combined. And he kept us informed. He and Mike competed in a seemingly continuous "Worst Joke" contest that gave them both no end of pleasure and us no end of grief.

Leigh had given up his family medical practice in town and was teaching at the community hospital up in Santa Rosa. He also did a lot of teaching on the trail — it just came naturally to him, and we were all eager to learn.

Bruce was at the high school then — math and physics — and we couldn't have prevented him from teaching if we'd tried. It was just in him, like coaching soccer was just him, and sailing his catamaran, and spending every minute he could with Anne and the kids. It was just him.

Rory was an arborist in Elgin, by far the best in town. He not only knew what he was doing, he knew why.

None of us had a greater appreciation for nature than Rory, and though some might have seen that as a conflict with his job, you only had to listen to him out on the trail to understand that it made perfect sense.

I was the sixth member of the original group. Soon after, we were joined by Matt Atkinson and Steve Camsi — both as solid as any guys you could ever want to meet. Matt had already retired from the park service and was working for an organic winery on the edge of town. Steve was a family therapist working part-time down in the city and full time on being a great husband and dad.

Somewhere along in there, somebody came up with the name. Slow Old Guys. SOGs. We weren't all that old then, really — and Rory and Leigh were anything but slow, but the name stuck instantly. It wasn't long before Jan made us Slow Old Guys tee shirts. We'd all wear them to the occasional organized runs we'd enter, and we'd collect the comments.

Mostly we would just run. There are great parks around Elgin. Not tight, groomed, city-block parks with swings and duck ponds. Real parks — acres of them with trails that wind through the hills and the chaparral in loops and circles that can take years, maybe a lifetime, to really get to know. We set out to do it.

And as we ran, we talked — about anything, everything. It wasn't just sports and remodeling and jobs, though there was plenty of that. And it wasn't about our wives, though for some folks who didn't know us, that was hard to believe. We talked about our families, yes, our town, sure. We talked about our kids as they grew older and began to separate from us — and our parents as they grew older and began to need us more. The crises and cares that came up in all our lives — a failed business, a family illness, sometimes just the blues.

We talked.

And when, near the end of May in the year 2000, Bruce died suddenly of a heart attack, the SOGs became something more.

All of us pulled together — closer — tighter. We needed it. God, how we needed it. We were there for Anne, for Joel and Carmen, for each other. We were there for ourselves.

Our Sunday mornings on the trails became more important. Some of our wives began to join us — starting out on a walk as we began our run. When one of us went on the "injured reserve" list with a bad knee or bad ankle, we joined them. Chuck named them the "Walkie-Talkies" — a name they instantly adopted with pride.

Bruce's death brought Ritch to the group. He was right: he and running didn't get along very well — particularly that first half mile. But he showed up the first Sunday after the memorial service and every Sunday after. He gutted it out until his lungs and legs stopped burning — and by sheer force of will, he got it done.

Without knowing exactly how, without even being aware of it as it was happening, we became an institution in our little town. And the weekly SOG runs became so much a part of our lives that none of us — no matter how old we could see ourselves becoming — could ever imagine not doing them. Nobody is in a wheelchair yet, but when the first one appears, the SOGs and the Walkie-Talkies will be joined by the Roly-polys who will no doubt keep on rolling to the last of their days.

Was the exercise important? Absolutely. Were the friendships important? Incredibly so. Just as important were the ideas. The trails on those mornings were a place where discussion was not only welcome, it was essential. A place where ideas had value. A place safe to think, to question, to dream.

But as President Trent said when he was inaugurated two years ago, "The careless dissemination of ideas that challenge the security we are fighting to maintain can be very dangerous to everything that all true and patriotic Americans hold dear."

From his perspective, he was absolutely right.

CHAPTER FIVE
TWENTY HOURS LEFT

WARDEN YEAGER IS a short man. While that was probably the first thing I noticed about him, it certainly wasn't the only thing. In three months, I have never known him to be late. Never known him to raise his voice. Never known him to wear anything but the same blue shirt, same gray suit jacket, same black tie. There is always a slight nervous air about him — though maybe that's not quite right. Timid maybe. Tentative is more like it. Reserved. Maybe even conflicted. But short for sure. Unusually short.

"Why, it looks like you have company." Zebel is standing at the door to my cell. "How nice for you. Good morning, Warden Yeager." He ushers the warden into my open cell door. "Mr. Davis has been a perfect gentleman this morning, as always

Yeager gives him a look — half a look — that I swear is exactly the look I would have given Zebel if I could. I don't dare — the guy scares me.

"Mr. Davis, please have a seat. I hope you don't mind if I sit at your desk. There are some questions I need to ask you . . . papers to fill out. It's just routine."

"Of course." I've moved back onto my bunk, put my back up against the wall, crossed my arms. "I can't imagine what you could still need to know, but I'm a captive audience. Fire away." I smile to myself at the sick joke — Mike and Chuck would be proud. Yeager isn't smiling.

I do my best to answer his questions. I swear to God, it's a customer satisfaction survey — the death row version. How have I been treated? How has the food been? Do I have any complaints or criticisms I would like passed on to prison authorities?

I guess it's all about the information. Maybe they need it, ridiculous as it is — maybe there's something of importance to uncover from the answers to these stupid questions. It is all part of the "Productive Penal Program" that Trent instituted when he took office

— a cornerstone of the Compassionate Corrections Corporation's efforts to sweep away the broken model and usher in a new era of fairness and efficiency, or at least efficiency. Maybe it is just the system covering its ass, asking me stupid questions that, in light of my short-term plans, have absolutely no relevance to me, probably less to them. But just having the information seems important to them — no matter what it is, no matter how obtained. The cameras in my cell aren't enough. Nor are the listening devices that I know are in the walls. So much information. Yet after all these years, they still don't seem to get that the data is worth nothing without the intelligence to understand it.

It began with the Justice Department, I think it was in 2002. The name they gave it was "Total Information Awareness," though it didn't take long for us to call it TIA. It was part of the big three: USA Patriot Act, Department of Homeland Security, and TIA. Three arms of our protective government ready to enfold us and make us secure. More like a three-headed snake. Three heads but one goal: fear.

Fear that somebody somewhere might be planning to do something awful to us. There *was* a real foundation for the fear. The World Trade Center was just the first in a series of attacks, and with every successive assault, the government tightened up more. The tighter it got, the more attacks and attackers squeezed out through the cracks.

We were assured that these new powers were required to protect us and would never be abused. Judgment would be applied, controls would be put in place, misuse of this new authority would be impossible under the system of review and oversight that had been carefully and rigorously imposed. I suppose by some definition somewhere, those statements might have been true.

TIA became law. Information poured in from credit cards and ATMs and computers and the internet and phone records and anything that could be tagged, tapped, or traced.

The fallout began almost instantly, though few noticed.

The enhancements to Megan's Law were the first wave. Though it seems quaint now, the law was revolutionary when it was first passed. Convicted sex offenders were put on a public registry and had to sign in with law enforcement wherever they went.

Controversial for its time — and calling into question the rights to privacy and free travel — it also raised serious constitutional issues about punishing a criminal after his sentence had been served. Yet the law was widely supported. Maybe even justified.

But under TIA it was possible to do more. The internet was still relatively young then, and child pornography had found a home in cyberspace. There could be no middle ground on child pornography — it simply wasn't okay. So when the TIA database was asked to identify all those who had clicked on a website with child pornography, it took no great leap of faith or logic to add those names to the sex offender registries. People had a right to know if some sick bastard was living next door. Of course, the sick bastard might never know he'd been listed, because under TIA there was no obligation to tell him. More common, though, were the houses vandalized at night, the bricks through windows, the jobs lost and leases canceled.

The next step was almost as easy. Megan's Law was enhanced again, not just to include those who visited child porn sites, but those who looked at ANY pornography on the web. The linkage back to the original intent of the law was clear and experts were found to certify that the pathology was the same. The registry swelled astronomically. And who but the ACLU would dare to raise a voice in protest? A few did, but not many. Not many at all, considering that pornography was the biggest moneymaker anywhere on the web.

But the lists didn't grow instantly. A six-month moratorium was instituted from the time the law was passed. Though the records of every click existed going back a couple of years, implementation of the law was delayed until there could be no doubt that anyone who might be implicated had been warned. And those old records, those old clicks on Trixie's Pleasure Palace — all erased. When the law took effect, everyone started with a clean slate, or so the government said.

In those six months, porno on the internet vanished. It was simply gone, relegated to cash only DVD rentals and imported magazines in brown paper wrappers.

Did security improve? No. Did crimes involving sex go down? No. But the Justice Department had a clear mandate, and they ran with it. TIA was alive and well — and the First Amendment went on life support.

Now Yeager is asking me, in his best voice so the hidden mikes can pick it up, if I would like to lodge any formal complaints about my treatment, as this will be our last "Evaluation Opportunity."

"I'll save my last statement for — what are you calling it now — the 'Final Processing Procedure?' Thank you for asking though." I stare at him. He looks away.

I turn my gaze to the camera in the corner of the ceiling, knowing full well that I cannot make it blink or turn away any more than I can make it understand.

CHAPTER SIX
NINETEEN HOURS LEFT

I REMEMBER 2002 as a bleak year for the country and for the SOGs. The elections that November were awful. As if the electorate was in a coma and Congress not only gutless but rudderless. President Bush behaved like a school bully who'd just been named Student of the Month. Clinton may have been the first "Quantum Politician" — able to be on both sides of an issue and squarely in the middle at the same time — but at least he understood that compromise was an essential part of his job. Bush was totally unfamiliar with the concept.

We ran every Sunday. We watched and read the news, alternately frustrated, disheartened and horrified.

The USA Patriot Act — with such a name who could possibly be against it — was both a law and a litmus test. The few in Congress who dared to question it — any of it — were as much as branded traitors. The implications were all too clear: The President said it every chance he got. "In this fight, you are either with us or against us. There is no middle ground." He was talking about the war on terrorism. What few realized was that his war would extend to all of us. We would all be asked to take sides, in large ways and small. Most Americans elected to go along.

The Department of Homeland Security also came into existence in 2002. It was an old business concept applied by old men to what they thought of as an old problem: too many chiefs, not enough Indians. Too much duplication of effort, too many competing interests. If only we could bring it all under one big tent. The independent departments vanished overnight with the press trumpeting triumphs and victories for the new organization. But the conglomerating mentality — that ultimately exploded one company after another in the merger boom of the late nineties — worked no better in government.

And TIA, Total Information Awareness, the Justice Department's darling, took on a life of its own. If there was a saving grace, it was that it became too big, too quick. A lumbering giant barely able to get out of its own way. You could stay mostly safe if you could stay unnoticed. People adapted quickly to invisibility. But if it got you in a corner, you were done.

Each of the SOGs was particularly offended by something. Our Sunday trail runs became a forum for our frustrations.

Leigh was working at Public Health then. We hadn't yet invaded Iraq, but it was a foregone conclusion that we would. We were told — with no supporting evidence —that Saddam had a secret cache of the smallpox virus.

Our president ordered the country vaccinated. Not all of it, not all at once (or so he said at the time). Leigh was clear: "If he can keep us afraid, he can keep us from thinking and from asking why." Mass vaccination was a ridiculous idea medically and uncalled for strategically. It proceeded just the same. The public was assured that nothing could go wrong. That several hundred of us might die if we weren't screened properly — might die even if we were screened — was never widely disclosed.

It wasn't a genuine panic that followed the initial announcements; the country seemed too nearly asleep for anything so dramatic as panic. But people were afraid. When it was discovered that some of the old vaccines had lost their potency and were no longer effective — and that there would not be enough to go around — the fear increased.

One of the things about our country that is undeniably true, even today, is that regardless of what happens, someone somewhere will figure out how to turn a profit on it. Almost instantly black-market vaccines hit the Internet and then the street. Most of them were nothing but a placebo. Though administered by mouth or patch, a needle prick of no utility was required, because it seemed more real. Harmless enough — if a batch of the bogus kits hadn't been contaminated with staph bacteria. Several thousands were infected, several hundred died. Bush claimed it was a terrorist plot. More fear.

For Mike Witkowski, the rollback of the fuel economy standards made no sense. For twenty years, cars really had been using less fuel. The first gas/electric hybrids were on the road, even a few all-electric cars. The air was getting cleaner every year.

The threat of war changed everything.

Almost overnight it became not only a lifestyle statement but a patriotic statement to drive something big, something American, something that burned gas like we would never run out. Mike kept searching for ways to explain the phenomenon to his students. When he tried telling the truth, he was slapped down — not just by some parents but subtly by the school district. Politics had entered the first grade.

Rory, whose outdoor work every day as an arborist put him in closer touch with the natural environment than any of us, kept trying to find some way to rationalize the *burn baby, burn* mentality — the notion that using more would somehow produce more — and just couldn't. It meant that drilling off the coast of California would almost certainly begin again. It meant that the Alaska National Wildlife Reserve, which had just been declared off-limits to drilling rigs, suddenly wasn't. Logical or not, the changes came quickly, and with what looked like broad support. In a choice between security — real or illusional — and anything else, the Americans made their preference clear.

Ritch Foster locked on the faith based charity" movement that jumped in to pick up after the cuts, curtailments, and complete abandonment of social service programs. The cost of such programs ate into the national security effort to balance the budget. Yet funds were doled out to any church that aspired to "good works." No details required.

For me it was guns. I just didn't understand them, not in the way most of the country seemed to. I read the Second Amendment. How could that simple statement about the right to form a militia and bear arms have turned into this holy crusade? It couldn't be about the guns themselves — that was too easy. Power maybe? Control? Security? Maybe a general feeling of impotence. Though Viagra was selling strong.

Rich Yonash considered moving to New Zealand. "The madness hasn't hit there. They see what we're doing and they just shake their heads."

Leigh and I looked at our local political parties. I went to a few County Democratic Central Committee meetings. Leigh tried Green Party get togethers. We compared notes. The Greens had better discussions, the

Dems had better food. Neither had the answers we were looking for, nor an avenue to find them.

We all felt lost. Maybe that is why Bush was getting his way, trading civil rights for the promise of security. Every day we were committed to a new deal with the devil. The few voices of protest went unheard.

I remember thinking that it wouldn't last, that the country of Jefferson and Lincoln, of Roosevelt and Kennedy, of King and Carter would wake up, and soon.

I remember thinking it was only a matter of time.

I have never been so wrong.

CHAPTER SEVEN
EIGHTEEN HOURS LEFT

FOR THE LAST HOUR, Zebel has just been watching me. Just watching. That's his job, I know, but this is different. I think maybe that *thing* lurking behind his eyes is trying to show itself.

And what's this? Before, he was watching like he was looking through me. Now he is absolutely watching ME, and I don't like it.

He is turning slightly in his chair, turning away from the camera in the hall. It can see him, of course, but now only his back. From somewhere in his clothing, he is fishing for something. A small revolver. No government-issue job — that's the big black one strapped in the holster on his belt. This gun is his. It isn't supposed to be here. That I know for sure.

Slowly — so the movement won't look suspicious to the camera at his back — he is raising the gun.

Barrel first. Putting it in his mouth. He motions with his finger on the trigger. And he motions with his eyes. An invitation?

"I know how sensitive you are about your privacy," he is saying as he stands, the gun concealed again. He says it nice and loud for the microphones, ensuring his words are recorded if anyone ever decides to listen. "If you need a moment, Mr. Davis," he's at the bars, the gun hidden in the palm of his extended hand, "I'll be glad to turn my back for you."

I will not let him get to me, or I'm damn sure not going to let him see that he has.

Yet he's done it.

For three months, I've been thinking about everything, anything but the one thing that I ultimately cannot avoid.

In less than eighteen hours, I'm going to die. I know about the appeals. I know about the possibilities. I know from a lifetime of learning that nothing is certain until it's certain.

I've never set out on a trip without some idea of where I might be going. Yet for three months all I've been thinking about is what I'll be leaving behind.

What is out there for me, if and when all else fails? I know that it does fail for all of us eventually. What comes after seems like a futile question. Rarely even posed, at least by me. I know that sounds a bit superior on my part, considering that mankind has spent all of recorded history, and probably everything that came before, wondering exactly that.

It was easy when I was a child. There were angels. There were fluffy white clouds. Seemed like a pretty good place. Yes, I knew there was another place that was not so pretty, and in spite of the fact that I was a very normal kid and did a lot of absolutely normal kid things that certainly classified as sins in somebody's book, I figured eventually the clouds would be mine.

When I was a teenager, reincarnation had the most appeal. My mom was into it. She read all the books and passed some of them along to me. Fun to think about having been some noble — but conveniently minor — historical figure reborn into our modern age. Fun to think about coming back again and again in different shapes. My favorite was a hawk. A soaring hawk. Not because it was fierce but because it could float on the wind. That sounded okay.

My grandparents talked of going to their "last reward." I knew it meant dying but never thought about what it really meant. I've been thinking about it lately — a last reward for a lifetime of living right. A last rest from all that toil. Not a bad image, that.

Nirvana, wholeness, perfect peace and harmony — now there is a popular notion. It's all in the Buddhist meditation books I've been reading lately. Right now, it's the exercises I'm interested in. Probably a little short-sighted, but there you are.

A state of grace? I don't know what that is exactly. It does sound good.

A higher power? I can go with that. In the years we've been married, Jan has often said that there are no accidents. Just as often, she's demonstrated it. But I've got to tell you: if there *is* some planning going on, there are still a few bugs in the system.

Absolutely nothing? I was there for a while. Maybe still am. Just blackness. Just nothing.

Years ago, Stedman probably pegged it as close as anybody — on one of our long, late-night drives. "You're a pantheist, Davis." We were trying to find a name for whatever it was I believed at the time. "You may not believe in God — or you may say you don't — but you see God in all things."

It sounded right when he said it.

It still does.

And what about death? We see it all around us — in nature, on the news, in person. I saw a kid die once. I was seven, he was a little older. He went over the handlebars on his bike and landed on his head. He was there one minute, then gone. Fast. Cold. Gone.

Maybe death isn't anything but the absence of life, but we sure feel the vacuum it leaves in its wake. All of us felt it when Bruce died — in our lives, in our hearts. Once we've been close to it, been touched by it, we react differently — on a personal level — whenever it comes near again.

But I still don't know what I think about it. Not for myself. Not for me.

Logically I know that the lights just go out. Yet I want there to be more. Maybe I'm just prime for a foxhole conversion.

Leigh could explain the pathology for me. He would do so gladly, if we had a chance to run again. But we won't.

Perhaps there is something else, though. I can convince myself that there is. Just a few times when I've meditated, I've felt something . . . something . . .

Zebel is staring, back in his chair now and staring. He knows I've forgotten him. He doesn't like it. Not at all. He wants to rattle me. He did there for a minute, but I'm okay now. I'm okay. Thinking of that place I've glimpsed.

Usually I close my eyes when I meditate, but I'm going to do it with them open now, staring right at him. I'll slow my breathing, relax, slow some more . . . release . . . and I'm almost there . . .

It's not Elgin this time. It's the woods, in the summer, in the evening.

Just ahead of me, just a little way ahead, there they are — the lights in the trees.

I'm almost there . . .

Chapter Eight
Seventeen Hours Left

THERE'S THE DOOR for the lunch-cart. A little late. Almost twenty after the hour, but what do I care? I'm not going anyplace — at least not for a while.

Critchett always eats what I eat for breakfast. If we have a bond, that's it. Zebel never does.

"Your lunch, Mr. Davis." He hands it through the slot in the bars, and I can see that they *did* get it right — turkey, cheddar, Dutch crunch roll — I can even smell the onions.

"I don't eat processed food, you know." He isn't looking at me as he plunges his fork into something that I can only assume is tofu. "You shouldn't either. That stuff'll kill you." His eyes are right on me now, and for a flash I see the demon in him. And the demon sees me. It is only the sound of the door opening at the end of the hall that sends it, reluctantly, back into hiding.

Stedman has visited my cell many times, but I have never been happier to see him than now. Zebel, silent, stands and opens the cell door for him.

As part of the kinder, gentler penal system reforms, virtually all news from the outside world is now kept from inmates, particularly those on death row. Only the clergy are allowed regular access. Not free necessarily but regular. In the early weeks of my incarceration, Steve and I actually kept up the pretense that he was a pastor. When our voices were raised, we still did. But in the cell in the quiet hour we got to spend together once a week, we soon relaxed and were just ourselves.

Every week I would get reports from him. There were the protests, the public appeals. Jan and Susan Reber went everywhere together — the widow of the murdered man and the wife of the man who killed him — always appearing side by side. The mainstream press barely covered their appearances, Steve explained, but the few alternative papers that were left did their best.

Then there was Ernie Joiner and the *Elgin Tribune*. Steve would recite Ernie's stories and editorials to me, almost word for word. Ernie wrote about the SOGs. He wrote about Jan and the kids, he wrote like his words might actually make a difference — and prayed that they would.

These three months I have received no letters and have been allowed no visitors but Steve. All these three months, all except yesterday. Jan and the kids yesterday. The bastards gave me just that one hour with them.

"Brother Wedgewood, how you holdin' up?" I was Wedgewood to Steve, had been for years. Neither of us could now recall why.

"Not holding up, Alberto . . . mostly just holding on

"Amen, brother. Amen

It has come down to this. There are only four ways I will get out of this cell. The first, requiring a right turn at the door, is a very short walk that will come to an abrupt end. While not a sure thing, that route is currently the odds-on favorite.

But there are three others. Steve and I will talk about them again today, each in turn, though we've been over it all before.

In just a few hours the Board of Directors of the Compassionate Corrections Corporation will hear an appeal on my behalf — and, strangely, on theirs. My legal team has learned that they are not at all pleased with the way my case was handled, meaning handled by someone other than themselves. They take no particular exception to the way things are going in general, and have no qualms about my eventual appearance in the Rust Room. But President Trent himself had become personally involved. Right from the start. In spite of the brand-new prison reforms he had championed and the new stack of rules and procedures, in my case Trent had simply done as he wished, not even bothering to consult them. Toes were stepped on. Many toes. Authorities were challenged. Rules — the almighty rules – had been broken by the score. The Compassionate Corrections Corporation's board valued their new power as much as they valued their rules and didn't much like Trent's interfering in territory they considered to be their own. They can't stop the execution, but just to exert a little control, they can slow it down, delay it until every comma and semicolon is positioned properly. Maybe a few days, maybe more. Probably nothing.

Then there are the Supremes. In spite of everything that has changed, they have held on to the power to stop it. Though so far, every argument brought before them has been rejected. It was Bush's court, now it's Trent's, and his war mentality seems to have blinded them. But there's still one chance, one approach that hasn't been tried. Can't be tried until now, this close to the end.

The third way out is no way at all. Trent, with a stroke of his pen, can commute my sentence to life. Why would he even consider that? Because of protests? Because of rumors, never officially confirmed, that polls are showing a softening of support for his administration and for him? But he won't do it. His image isn't built around letting go. He can't allow it to look like he is caving to pressure. Even if he feels it, he can't show weakness. Can't even hint that he's afraid he's gone wrong. My last-minute appeal for clemency is moving quickly through the appropriate channels, but nobody is taking odds that it will get very far.

Fifty-eight years of life comes down to this: my fate decided by a room full of bureaucrats I've never met, a room full of tired old men and women in black robes, and a guy who, publicly at least, says I'm as bad as Bin Laden.

"Wedgwood, old son," we are standing now as Steve gets ready to leave. "Just remember, it ain't over till the fat lady sings." He puts his arms around me, hugs me close, and in my ear whispers, ". . . and maybe it ain't even over then."

Chapter Nine
Sixteen Hours Left

"WHAT ARE YOU smiling about, Davis?"

Not Mr. Davis anymore, just Davis. And he's caught me smiling.

"I was just thinking about the NRA." I'm smiling more now that I've verbalized what I was remembering. "Surprised?"

"A little." Zebel actually looks a bit off guard. "Considering that you've got an intimate date with ten card carrying members in just a little over fifteen hours."

"I suppose I do." My smile just won't fade. "Do you suppose it will make any difference if they know I'm a member, too . . . or used to be? Probably not. Just the same, I guess I shouldn't have let that membership lapse."

Strange as it may seem now, in light of the direction things have taken in the last eight years, there was no chapter of the NRA in Elgin in 2003. Stranger, there was no chapter in all of Sonoma County, not an active one anyway. A charter had been issued back in the seventies, but membership had dwindled as the organization's goals changed. I guess ours wasn't the NRA's kind of a county.

It was Mike Witkowski who came up with the idea on one of our trail runs. We all watched what the NRA had done in the aftermath of the Columbine shootings. We couldn't believe it, but we watched and read and watched them do it again and again. Their manipulation of the political process had become so well refined that they no longer attempted to hide it. They boasted publicly as one legislator after another fell in line. They were good at playing on people's fears.

From my cold, dead hands had gone from being a motto to a mantra said everywhere they went.

But they were a democratic organization and proud of it. Governed by policies and bylaws, subject to the will of their voting members, they even held what could only be described as political conventions to elect officers and adopt platforms. It was Mike who learned that the NRA

National Congress for 2003 was in Anaheim, right next to Disneyland.

All our good ideas came on Sunday runs. "Maybe we're viewing this gun thing all wrong." Mike had just told an awful joke, and we were half expecting another one. "The NRA isn't like death or taxes. They are not inevitable. Maybe they can be changed."

Nobody was laughing.

"They hold elections, don't they? They have conventions, pass bylaws, issue policy statements. Instead of always complaining about what they're up to, why don't we join them and take over?"

I can't remember which one of us pointed out the fact that, on that particular morning, there were only five of us SOGs on the trail and as many Walkie-Talkies elsewhere in the park. "Mike, if everybody we knew joined up, those regular NRA guys would still only outnumber us by a hundred thousand to one."

"Sure, nationally. But right here in Elgin, I bet we'd comprise the majority, maybe the whole membership. And we could vote for our delegate representatives to the national convention."

Suddenly we all understood.

It felt strange sending money to the NRA. The membership dues weren't much, and we knew that we'd only be paying them once. We sent in the forms, and Mike took care of reactivating the dormant county chapter. All by phone, fax, and e-mail. We kept it as quiet as we could, but Ernie Joiner somehow tumbled to what we were planning. None of us knew Ernie all that well back then, but he pretty much made us an offer we couldn't refuse.

"I'm going with you guys," he told us over beers down at Murphy's one night. He didn't state it as an idea and certainly not as a request. It was just a fact, and because he had a press pass, there would be no problem getting him in.

Six of us loaded into Mike's van and headed south. Ernie told us stories of his days on the big city papers. He was about twenty years our senior, not old enough to be a father figure but certainly a favorite uncle. That trip was the beginning of our mutual adoption.

We drove straight through, got a couple of rooms, and showed up to the warm welcome of our fellow members: the brand-new delegation from Elgin, California. For most of those in attendance, Elgin was as alien as the backside of the moon. "I thought it was mostly pansy pickers and tree huggers up that way," somebody actually said. Six heads nodded.

The first day was primarily mixers and seminars. Mike was warmly received as the chairman of our new chapter. Even without our suggestion, he was asked to say a few words at the general assembly the next day. He humbly accepted the invitation.

For the remainder of that day, we walked the tradeshow floor. As part of my job, I'd been attending tradeshows for years, but never one like this. If it could shoot, it was there. If you could imagine it, somebody just down the aisle probably had it. Gun heaven, wall to wall.

At every booth where we found something of particular interest, the salespeople were always delighted to loan us samples when we explained that they'd be part of the main presentation the following day.

We collected all the props we needed.

Back in our rooms that night, we felt like we were bivouacked in an armed camp. We could hardly sleep for all the deadly hardware stashed in the closets and under the rollaway beds.

The next day, we were on first, right after the pledge and the national anthem. The outgoing chairman introduced all the dignitaries, called the Congress to order, and then we were up. "I would now like to introduce Mr. Mike Witkowski, president of the newly reactivated Sonoma County chapter." There was an audible sound of disbelief from throughout the room, so he had to repeat it. "Ladies and Gentlemen, please welcome the face of the *new* NRA!"

The place went mildly wild. Sonoma County apparently had a reputation. We were also a fair bit younger than the average attendee, so we must have looked pretty good to them.

Maybe we really were the face of the new NRA.

Mike strode to the podium. We flanked him on either side.

"This is a rifle," he began, and he held aloft a long-barreled flintlock musket reproduction, circa

1770. A cheer exploded from the assembly — this was what they had come for. "When our sacred Second Amendment became law, this was the gun the framers knew." The cheers grew louder. "This was the gun they used to defend themselves on the frontier, to protect their homes, to free themselves from the tyranny of the British." Mike was almost shouting into the microphone now. It didn't seem to matter what he was saying as long as he brandished that gun. "When well-regulated militias were formed to insure the security of our new country, THIS RIFLE was the arm that they had a right to bear and keep.

"THIS RIFLE," he raised it again, and the assembly was on its feet.

"THIS RIFLE!"

He lowered his arm, lowered the gun. It came up again with a Mac-10 automatic assault weapon Leigh had handed him. "Not this one." He lowered it, we switched guns. The crowd was still cheering but not quite so loudly.

"And not this one." A modified M16.

"Not this one." He raised another automatic.

"Not this one." Another.

The cheers had vanished.

"This rifle" – he raised the musket one last time – "is what the Second Amendment of our constitution is about. The Elgin California chapter of the National Rifle Association thinks it is what the NRA should be about. Thank you."

Absolute silence now.

We set down our props and passed out through the parting crowd like Moses through the Red Sea.

We spent the rest of the day at Disneyland.

But Ernie Joiner stayed. His press pass didn't say where he was from. He stayed, and he wrote, and he ran Mike's speech word for word on the front page of his next edition. There was Mike's picture, the musket held aloft, and a caption that read, "From their cold, closed minds."

He was the editor — he could do as pleased with his little out-of-the-way paper in our little out-of-the-way town. But the nationals picked up the story and ran it with his byline — and the caption and photo eventually made their way to the cover of Newsweek.

Ernie had a little extra spring in his step for a good long while after that.

CHAPTER TEN
FIFTEEN HOURS LEFT

THE ONE AND ONLY time they let me see Jan and the kids was twenty-four hours ago. I don't know why they allowed it. It violates every tenet of the new policy for death row prisoners — but that's not my problem. For all the hours since then, I've been trying to keep the memory of that visit walled off. Not because the memory isn't good. It is too good. And it's the last one. And in this awful place, I want to protect at least that memory, since I can no longer protect them or myself.

But it's no use. I miss them too much not to see them one more time, even if only in my mind.

The cell felt so small with the four of us crowded in together. No visiting room for the likes of me, no going off the block until the final departure. Zebel sat in the hall, watching the whole time, probably glaring.

I didn't check. The minute they were with me, they were all I could see.

Emily was great. She wore the old "No Fear" sweatshirt we bought together all those years ago, and on the inside of her palm she'd written in blue pen, "Fuck 'em if they can't take a joke!" She is twenty-six now, doing commercial art because she's good at it and private art because it makes her happy. Occasionally she writes a movie review for Joiner's paper — without exception they are damned good.

Noah talked the most —it was like music listening to him. That's how Noah relates to the world: he talks — not at it, but to it, with the same open enthusiasm and energy for everybody. It's fitting that sound is how he makes his living. "Sound is the only language that we all understand," he said to me once. No one taught him that, he just knew it. It's in the movies he's worked on and the spoken word recordings. Lately, the underground audio files coded to defy government trace and full of truths rarely spoken openly now. All of them bear his unmistakable mark. Thirty years old. A good man. A good friend.

When she wasn't hugging me, Jan mostly cried quietly or laughed or both at once. Jan. I have never known anyone stronger or more vulnerable. There are no half measures with Jan. Unconditional love is not an abstraction for her — it's what she does. I can't imagine what these three months have been like for her, but I know what she's been doing virtually non-stop. Appearances, appeals, pleas. Stedman has kept me informed. But without being told, I would have known anyway. Jan could do nothing less. It just isn't in her.

The four of us had the best time in spite of everything. We talked, remembered, laughed, wept. Emily brought me my old dog-eared copy of *The Complete Sherlock Holmes*, and Noah had the Tolkien trilogy with him. From long experience, they knew that I reread them both every couple of years. They said it was probably time to start again.

I got to embrace each of them one last time. What a gift to hold a beautiful young woman in your arms. And know she's your daughter and she's extraordinary and the world's a better place because she is in it. What a gift to feel the strength of your son's arms around you and to lean on him and feel him carry your weight — and know that he will carry on.

Jan was the last, and she wouldn't let go.

She will never let go.

Footsteps in the hallway again now, footsteps pulling me back. Probably Yeager. Why now?

"Mr. Zebel." Yeager is addressing the guard like he addresses all his guards, but I notice he isn't standing very close to him, and he seems a bit tenser than usual. "I would like you to step to the far end of the hall for a moment."

No response from Zebel. Not at first, though for a second I almost think the demon might show itself. But a request from Yeager is an order, and Zebel moves away slowly.

"Mr. Davis." Yeager has his back to Zebel and, I realize, to the cameras. He repeats my name softly, drawing me closer to where he stands next to the bars. "A representative from President Trent is in my office. There may be a way out of this for you if your remaining appeals fail. I will be contacted again if that time comes, and I will contact you. Under the right circumstances,

President Trent may be willing to commute your sentence to life. You may still have a chance to see them again." He is looking straight at me, and I know without a doubt that he knows exactly what I was remembering just before he arrived.

"You're serious." It's not so much a question as a statement. He is never anything but serious, yet I can hardly believe it.

"He is in my office right now. You have two appeals pending, but I've been authorized to tell you that if you withdraw them right now, I will be given the President's terms right now. You could end this. But not if word gets out." He glances over his shoulder at Zebel, who appears not to be listening but obviously is. "We know about Stedman. I want you to be clear on this point: if word of the offer gets out, it was never made."

How can they be doing this? How? Is it some final punishment? One final lifeline to be jerked away at the last minute? Is it even sincere? I look at Yeager. He's watching me, waiting. It is real, or at least Yeager thinks so. He may be many things, but a liar isn't one of them.

"I still have two appeals left," I hear myself saying. "Tell Trent's man that I'll think about it. Tell him I need to let the appeals run their course. Tell him, crazy as it sounds and broken as it is . . . I still think the system might actually work."

CHAPTER ELEVEN
FOURTEEN HOURS LEFT

IN EARLY AUTUMN of 2004, the SOGs took their next step — the one that ultimately landed me here, I suppose.

For reasons I can no longer remember, all five seats on the Elgin City Council were up for grabs that November. It was Joiner who suggested an all SOG ticket. Sure, he wanted to sell some papers. But mostly I think he liked our style. We'd gained some notoriety from our foray into the NRA, and Ernie figured we should run with it.

But it was Rich Yonash ¬— my boss and lifelong friend — who made up my mind. Rich had flirted with moving to New Zealand. In the end, he concluded, "We all have the right to bitch and bellyache, but only because we were born here. I think maybe it's time for some of us to shoulder the responsibility that comes with that right. If you and your running buddies have the stomach to go for it, I'll help any way I can."

The campaign slogan was simplicity itself: "Run with the SOGs." And run we did. We ran all over our little town for several weeks leading up to the election. We agreed not to raise any money, or at least no more than the legal filings would require. Aside from pounding the pavement, our main campaign strategy was a simple handwritten letter. Each of us wrote to twenty acquaintances. We were careful not to overlap, so a total of a hundred letters went out in that first batch. We explained who the SOGs were, though most folks around town already knew us or at least knew someone who did. We explained that we were running for the council because we felt a responsibility to make a difference. We asked the recipient to write a similar letter to twenty of their friends if they agreed that we deserved a shot.

Not everybody wrote that second letter, not even half. But in a town with only five thousand people, it wasn't long before pretty much every mailbox had received at least one. By a week before the election, many of those who *hadn't* received a letter made it clear that they felt slighted. That was an invitation: we ran by their houses on that final Sunday morning and dropped them off in person.

In truth, it wasn't much of a race. Only three of the five seats were contested. One candidate dropped out as soon as we signed on, and the other two never bothered to campaign at all.

The same thing seemed to be happening in most small towns — and some that were not so small. Voter turnout was low and getting lower. People weren't stepping up to stand for office, and those who did often shouldn't have. The candidate pools were getting shallower and shallower — from big ponds all the way to little puddles like ours. Who could blame those who stayed away? It was open season on elected officials, had been for years. Everyone was frustrated with politics in general, and the venom that frustration created was directed at any officeholder within reach.

Who needed that kind of aggravation?

Who wanted the abuse?

Even though our city council race was virtually won before we started, Leigh convinced us all that we owed it to ourselves and to the community to sponsor a series of public forums. Sure, we could talk about local issues: sewer fees and tree ordinances and design reviews that make up the bulk of what a city council does. But Leigh insisted we owed the community more.

On four successive Saturday afternoons in the pavilion down at Ives Park in the heart of town, we set up tables, sat at microphones, and talked. Anybody who wanted to spend the time was welcome to attend. No subject was off-limits. We had our fair share of local complaints and gripes, but we also engaged in some real discussion, some genuine debate, some honest discourse.

We talked about ideas.

We weren't all on the same page on every issue. That was okay. In fact, our ability to respectfully disagree was what Ernie Joiner found so refreshing about us. He covered every forum and endorsed us without qualification. He did it because it was news in our little town, news he wanted to cover. It also didn't hurt that his circulation continued to rise.

So it was, on the first Tuesday in November 2004, that Mike Witkowski, Rory Pool, Ritch Foster, Leigh Hall, and Ed Davis were elected by a landslide to fill the five open vacancies on the Elgin City Council.

We had the best wishes of our friends.

We had a built-in majority.

We had favorable press.

And among us, we had barely a clue about what to do next.

CHAPTER TWELVE
THIRTEEN HOURS LEFT

IT IS JUST after 4 p.m. now, and already Stedman is at my cell door again.

"The Compassionate Corrections Corporation board turned us down, Wedge, but that doesn't mean anything. It was the longest shot we had. We've known that from the beginning."

"They've all been long shots, Steve. That's what we've known from the beginning. How many executions have been delayed by appeal since Trent took office? Exactly none. That's not just a coincidence — it's the platform he ran on — *Justice Delayed is Justice Denied.*

There were other planks in his platform, but that had been a big one, right along with the right to own as many guns as you wanted, of any kind you wanted. And, paradoxically, the right to life.

The Federal Penal System was a mess when Trent made his run for president. Sentences had grown longer and longer as one "get tough" administration followed another. Jails were overflowing. Prisoners, many of them innocent, were rotting in their cells, because their appeals were not being heard. Someone might have looked at the situation and wondered what so many people were doing in jail. Not Trent. To him it was simply a matter of efficiency. And, oh yes, humanity.

The changes he implemented once he took office were deceptively simple. In non-capital cases, when a sentence was issued, a clock started ticking. For a ten-year sentence, a ten-year clock. Any time an appeal was entered, the clock would stop ticking, and it would stay stopped until the appeal was resolved. Win the appeal and you might get a retrial, even win your freedom. Lose the appeal and the clock started up again right where it left off. An unsuccessful appeal that took six months to play out added six months to your sentence.

You were free to appeal as often as you liked.

For capital cases, there was another sort of clock — one that could not be stopped.

Any and all death penalty appeals were absolutely allowed and encouraged — it was every citizen's right to appeal what they believed to be an unfair judgement against them. But just because they'd filed an appeal, there was no reason to expect the clock to stop. If the courts were so backed up that those appeals could not be heard within the time allowed? Again, Trent had a simple answer. By executive order he appointed more judges, hundreds and hundreds of them, all prior-approved by his office and automatically confirmed upon nomination with Congress's rubber stamp.

The courts would be open twenty-four hours a day if necessary. Every appeal deserved to be heard. But they weren't, of course. They couldn't be. There was simply not enough time. Most of those that were considered ended up in front of *Trent's Boys*, as the new appointees were dubbed by defense lawyers. They *were* mostly boys, hardly a woman among them. And they were undeniably Trent's.

Many federal judges resisted the new procedures, incensed at the intrusion into their courtrooms and indignant that outside pressure was being applied by a

competing branch of government. Trent understood —
separation of powers was important. He immediately
separated all federal funding from any judge who was
troubled by the new involvement of the executive branch.

Judicial resistance to Trent's new policies vanished.

The National Bar Association never saw it coming,
couldn't see that the practice of law as they knew it in
our country had changed virtually overnight. It has
been two years since Trent took office, and they are still
mostly on their heels.

The ACLU continues to fight, of course, continuously
everywhere they can. But in controlling the courts all
the way to the top, Trent has effectively blunted their
arguments before they can even be made.

Where is Congress in all of this, you might wonder?
Simply running scared. During the Bush years, every
regressive proposal sent to the rank and file of both
houses won almost immediate approval. It was political
suicide otherwise — societal suicide for going along. As
terror attacks increased, there were arrests for newly
minted categories of criminals: Hostile Combatant,

Hostile Alien, Hostile Civilian. True, some legislators eventually began to question what they'd done.

By then it was too late.

As fear spread, the country grew more fragmented. Single issue political parties edged out the dissolving Democrats and Republicans. Now the AARP Party has as many members as all of the others combined — the AFLCIO Party, the NAACP Party, the NOW Party, the Right to Life Party, the Right to Choose Party, the Green Party, even the USA Patriot Party.

And finally, calling themselves what everyone understood they had become — the National Rifle Association Party.

At the end of Bush's second term, the political landscape looked like chaos — or maybe just fear masking as disorder. That was when Trent saw his opportunity. He promised stability. The trains, in effect, would once again run on time. As a starting place, the human cesspools that our prisons had become would be cleaned up, sanitized.

Professional.

Humane.

Justice would no longer be delayed because of a broken system that tortured its charges with years of delays before finally killing them. We were already killing them pretty fast even then in every state, every day. Trent simply added efficiency to a system that was hungry for it. When I landed here, he'd been in office almost two years and the death-row backlog was mostly cleared, so I've got this private wing all to myself. I have President Trent and his prison reforms to thank for it.

"Wedgewood, it's up to the Supremes now," Steve is saying, talking quietly, calmly. "You know they couldn't hear this final appeal until all the others had failed. But every one of those failures has made your case that much stronger."

I appreciate what he's doing but know it for exactly what it is. "Why will this one be any different, Alberto? They were Bush's judges, now they're Trent's. Why should they change direction?"

"Because they are still some of the best legal minds in the country, regardless of how they got there, and we only need a majority. On some level, each of those old farts still has respect for the Constitution they swore to uphold — not the mockery that's been made of it lately, but the real deal. For them, this is no longer about you. That brief your team is presenting right now is probably the shortest ever submitted to the Supreme Court, and it might just be the most important."

I had seen the brief. It consisted of a single page on which were written two words: "Due Process." It was an inspired and desperate gamble by the ACLU team that was representing me. One that, in the abstract, I had to admire. The mechanisms of the law might be complex, but the principles of justice were simple. Without due process, there could be no justice.

"Albert, do you really think that the very people who made it possible to deny me due process in the first place are going to reverse themselves and stop the hands on the timepiece over there?"

"It's not just you that's been denied, Wedge. We all have — the whole friggin country. If they turn away from you, they turn away from all of us and from themselves. I can't let myself believe they will turn away."

His words echo in the empty cellblock.

Echo and mix with the not quite silent ticking of
the clock.

CHAPTER THIRTEEN
TWELVE HOURS LEFT

5 P.M. CHANGE OF SHIFT. There are a lot of people on this planet who I would very much like to see again. Zebel isn't one of them. At least I won't have to after tonight.

Both Zebel and I hear the door opening at the end of the hall — the new guard coming on. Standing up from my cot too quickly, I feel a little dizzy and lean on the bars for support.

Zebel is right in my face.

"I heard what Yeager said," he is whispering. Obvious relish. "Now you hear me. You take that deal, and I'll make sure word gets out. Then they'll kill you twice if they can figure out how. I've got a date with my big screen TV in just twelve hours." He is hissing as he whispers. Without wanting to, I look into his eyes.

The demon is there, up front. "I'll be eating breakfast . . . scrambled eggs with lots of ketchup . . . and watching your brains splatter all over that back wall. And when the cameras finally cut to . . ."

"*Are you alright*, Mr. Davis?"

Zebel has a hold on me thorough the bars. I can't seem to find the strength to resist him.

"Mr. Davis, are you alright?"

Zebel lets go. "You're early, aren't you?" He shoots Cervantes a look. A threat really. The other man doesn't budge.

"Mr. Zebel, your shift is over now," Cervantes says very calmly. I see Zebel watching Cervantes's hand as it moves slowly towards the revolver on his hip. I'm really hoping Cervantes can see Zebel's hand doing the same.

And then the demon slides back in its hole.

"I'll be *seeing you*, Mr. Davis," Zebel says as he leaves. He has made clear exactly what he means.

"*Are* you alright, Mr. Davis?" Cervantes says again, quietly, when Zebel is gone. I want to say that I am alright. I want to BE alright. Suddenly I'm anything but.

It isn't just Zebel's eyes that have rattled me — it is what he wants to do with them less than twelve hours from now. He wants to watch me die. Wants to. How many more are there just like him? How many more are looking forward to seeing my life blasted out the back of my head? I keep trying to get my mind around the logic of it, the "why" of it. But I can't. I've known for three months exactly what is going to happen to me. I've even come to believe it, but I still don't understand.

Zebel is sick — that's at least an excuse of sorts. But what about the others?

What about all those others?

During his campaign, when Trent announced that federal executions would be televised, his poll numbers shot up fifteen points. That was when the NRA Party endorsed him, and the USA Patriots, and finally the moderate Republicans, though the conservative core of their party had relegated them to virtual insignificance by then. Trent and his backers from the far right were clearly in the driver's seat, clearly going to win. Endorsing him was the expedient way for moderates to get back into the game. It was sick political logic, but logic at least.

That people want to watch me die defies logic. People I don't know. Worst of all, people who bear me no ill will. They aren't a majority, but rule in our country hasn't required a majority for decades. The ideal of democracy is that every citizen has a vote and a responsibility to use it and that every vote counts. The reality, as practiced in this first decade of the twenty-first century, is that only a third of those who are eligible to register do so, and only a third of those who register actually vote. If half of those agree on anything, it's a landslide and becomes the law for all.

Tomorrow morning a sickening, heartbreaking number of the small group that is now in charge will be watching GBS. They will be watching me. Try as I might, I just do not understand, can't understand . . . can't seem to catch my breath . . .

"Mr. Davis." Cervantes is reaching through the bars to touch my shoulder. "Mr. Davis!"

"I don't feel well, Mr. Cervantes." My breathing is short, shallow, sweat jumping out on my forehead, forearms . . . heart pounding.

"I can't catch my breath." Calm . . . I've got to be calm . . . to slow down . . . got to breathe . . . be at peace . . . find that place . . . someplace . . . anyplace where I can hide from the millions of eyes that want to watch me die.

I'm reaching for it . . . reaching . . .

And it won't come.

CHAPTER FOURTEEN
ELEVEN HOURS LEFT

GOD, I FEEL TERRIBLE.

God, I need to use the john.

I'd been here two months before I realized why I always waited until early evening to use the toilet — really use it. Critchett and Zebel like to watch, especially Zebel. Mr. Cervantes always tries to find a way not to.

"Mr. Cervantes, I'm sorry, but I need to use the toilet."

"That's fine, Mr. Davis." And just like he has every other time, he turns sideways to me, not so much that the camera will think he isn't watching but enough so that I know he isn't.

A moment of privacy, such as it is.

The rim of the bowl is as cold as ever, but I feel better . . . slowly better.

Thank you, God and Mr. Cervantes, for this small courtesy in this awful place.

For the SOGs and for Elgin, our first year in office was a disaster. They say that anybody who appreciates good government — and anybody who likes good sausage — should never watch either being created. We weren't even close to making good government that first year. We knew it, but it was a bloody mess just the same.

The details of running a small town would seem to be simple enough, and I suppose maybe they can be. They sure weren't for us. Just getting a handle on the rules was hard — the formality, the protocols, the trappings of governance. Imagine trying to quarterback a football team if you've only ever watched from the sidelines. We felt like our first quarter was nearly over before we even understood the purpose of the game.

The first thing we learned, and we learned it quick, was that in government, big or small, it is the permanent staff that either gets the job done or makes it impossible to do anything at all. Fortunately for us, we had the former. Fortunately for the city of Elgin, our staff kept things running while we tried to learn how to distinguish our butts from a bucket of hot rocks.

At every meeting, we had a faithful crew of professional council watchers to remind us of what a terrible job we were doing. More like professional complainers. Their sole purpose on the planet seemed to be to make our lives as miserable as humanly possible. If anybody had been keeping score that first year, the Greek Chorus, as we came to call them, would surely have come out way on top.

Then there was the budget — or more properly, budgets. Every single damn thing had its own funding and expense tables and account codes and Christ knows what all else. One lesson became crystal clear — if given a choice between voting for a council member who claims to understand the budget and one who doesn't, vote for the second guy — because the first one is lying through his teeth.

It was mostly just crap that first year. Just crap.

We did pass a few resolutions, though. At least that felt good amid the general agony.

We declared ourselves a Nuclear Free Zone. We took a stand on renewable energy. We outlawed helium balloons (birds apparently choke on them, though

I was never so sure about that one). We sent letters to Washington about global warming, we sent letters about a lot of things. And we joined a few other cities around the country, a precious few, in passing resolutions in opposition to the USA Patriot Act and its helpmate, TIA. Those two resolutions were the best by far.

Some of us worried about being irrelevant. The sign somebody hung at the entrance to town declaring Elgin to be a "Common Sense Free Zone" didn't help much. But we knew, or at least believed, that our symbolic actions had value, even if they did nothing more than get people to talk.

As to running the city in that first year, the cartoonist Walt Kelly summed it up best: we had met the enemy, and he was us.

Chapter Fifteen
Ten Hours Left

DINNER IS HERE, and amazingly — I feel like I can eat it.

The people in my life love me. I make no mistake about that. Have never doubted it for a minute. But I've also taken no end of grief about my love of meatloaf and mashed potatoes — the undisputed king of comfort food. Nothing else is even in the same class.

First there are the thick slices of the meatloaf itself, rich with spices and warm enough that just a little steam rises when it's served. Add an indelicate mound of white, whipped potatoes on the side, and you've got perfection. The green beans are a concession to health, I know, but over the years, I've actually come to like them, too.

"Mr. Cervantes, please join me in a meal." I motion to his tray as I dig into mine. They've forgotten my beer, or maybe not forgotten. Maybe one final punishment, but that's okay. The meatloaf makes everything okay.

My guard has not moved from his position in the hall. "I know you like it, Mr. Cervantes. I remember from the one other time they served meatloaf. Please."

"I'm sorry, Mr. Davis," he says, distracted. Quieter than usual. "I don't seem to have an appetite tonight — but, please, enjoy yours."

I don't require any encouragement. But as I eat, I can't help but look at him. A handsome Hispanic man, slight of build, about my height. Trim, self-contained — like Critchett in that physical way, but in that way only.

And tonight, he's something else.

He's troubled.

I'm sure of it.

As a city council, we muddled through that first year. In the beginning of our second year, we started to jell. Found our footing. Though none of us knew it at the time, we found what we'd been looking for during a budget meeting. The department heads, such as they were (a few people wear many hats in a little town like ours), were going through their lists of funding requests.

Sanitation needed a new garbage truck.

The clinic needed new exam tables. And a new front door, because somebody had kicked a hole in the old one. No one knew precisely why.

Maintenance and Operations needed a new truck, new tools. Always more tools.

Dave Reber, our police chief, was extraordinary. Hard to describe him — big of frame, bigger of heart. He could be gentle and fierce and both at once if the job required it. Thankfully, in Elgin, the fierce rarely got trotted out.

His appearance before the council was never perfunctory. Dave's politics were well to the right of mine — but way left of anything going on in Washington. He was a formidable debating opponent, a worthy adversary, and a great guy to have a beer with afterwards.

"Honorable city council members," he began that particular night, "I come before you with a simple request. The firearms that my small force and I find ourselves forced to carry, while not being antiques exactly, would certainly not be out of place in many a fine museum. I'm afraid that my private, though modest, collection at home is not only newer in the aggregate but is in far better condition than the sidearms our officers find themselves strapped with . . . if you'll pardon the pun. I humbly submit that it's about time we get some new guns, fellas. These are pretty shot . . . pardon again."

He gave us a number for what the guns would cost, and a motion had already been made and seconded when Leigh said, "Wait . . . wait . . .Why do you need them?"

It was a simple enough question, but Reber didn't seem to hear.

"Why do our police officers need guns at all?" Leigh repeated. And Dave — for the first time in our experience on the council — was speechless.

But not for long.

"We need them because we are POLICEMEN." Had there been a soap box handy, he would have vaulted right up onto it. "I know you fellows are new to your jobs, so here's how it works. Bad guys do bad things. Cops are good guys. We try to apprehend the bad guys whenever we can. Sometimes we need a gun."

"When?" Leigh was leaning forward in his chair now. We all were. Something was coming. "When do you need a gun?" Leigh asked. "How often? When was the last time that you . . . that ANY of our officers drew his gun in the line of duty, let alone fired it?"

"That's not the point," Dave began. "The point is . . ."

"When?" Leigh could be direct when he needed to. "I want to know when."

Reber took a deep breath. "I wasn't prepared for the question, and off the top of my head, I can't recall. If you like, I'll examine our files prior to the next meeting so I can answer more precisely, but . . ."

"Chief Reber." Mike Witkowski now. "I've lived in this town for thirty years. You have too. In all that time, I can't remember a single incident when a gun was fired by one of our officers . . . and neither can you."

It was obvious from the look on Dave Reber's face that Mike was right.

The motion was withdrawn and a new one introduced. By a vote of five to zero, the Elgin City Council voted to remove guns from our police force. Further, we voted to sell the guns we had. And the ammunition. And to use the proceeds to replace the clinic door.

It was a nice piece of work.

When the meeting was adjourned and Dave was leaving the council chambers, he said, not under his breath at all, "Well I'll be fucked."

It wasn't two weeks later, on a domestic disturbance call, that Dave very nearly was fucked. And fucked for good.

As he related the story to us at the next council meeting, he was the first officer on the scene. Rosie Pinola had called the hotline to say that her boyfriend was beating her, that she needed help, that he had a . . . but the dispatcher couldn't hear the rest.

"I got to the house" – Dave's delivery to us was surprisingly calm, considering – "and I was sure this bastard — pardon me — the suspected perpetrator had a piece and was laying for me. I, as you know, had no piece whatever. Only that's not exactly true. Your vote last month said we couldn't carry real guns. It didn't say anything about look-alikes. I had one in the glove box just in case. From inside the house, it sounded like somebody was getting seriously fucked over . . . pardon me. Anyway, I grabbed my dummy gun and hit the door at a dead run.

"The first thing I saw was a shape in the corner with a piece leveled right at me. And I fired, just that quick. It wasn't a dummy gun in my hand, not in my mind anyway. I just let him have it.

"The him, as you know, was one Enrique Pinola, age seven, who I am happy to say is alive and well. Not thanks at all to me. You are responsible for saving that kid's life. And for saving mine from what shooting him would have certainly done to me."

We all knew right then, all of us, that in our little council room, in our little town, we had done something good, something right, something that made a difference. Our actions really did matter. They had consequences. They might — just might — be able to influence others' actions as well.

At the very least, a tragedy had been averted, and all our lives were a little better for it.

We had done a good thing.

We wanted to do more.

CHAPTER SIXTEEN
NINE HOURS LEFT

IT WON'T BE LONG now, a couple of hours at most, before Ernie Joiner gets to spend an hour with me for one last interview.

One last visit.

Ernie is our only honorary SOG — too old to run, too cranky even to consider it. He couldn't help but admire what we were trying to do in Elgin, even if he didn't always agree. Honorary or not, intentional or not, Ernie helped us discover our voice as a group. And in the process, we somehow helped him rediscover his conscience.

Our next few years in office were good ones. We tried some things. Ernie supported our actions editorially when he could, opposed them when he couldn't, gave us fair coverage no matter what.

It pissed him off no end that we continued to run together every Sunday morning. We had to endure more than one editorial diatribe about holding private meetings. Doing the public's business *in public* was a major hobbyhorse for Ernie — and a good one, set in law with the Brown Act. To settle him down and keep the State of California off our backs, we began posting our Sunday runs as public meetings. The agenda: "Four miles in the Regional Park, followed by bagels at Shone's." Far from mollifying him, it pissed him off even more.

When the SOGs weren't making news in Elgin, the *Tribune's* coverage ran to the sorts of things you'd expect to see in a small-town newspaper. The quality of the writing was a little better than most, the quality of the photos a little poorer than the major daily's, but Ernie had nothing to be ashamed of. Every now and again he would get a little sensational in his reporting — his formative years spinning out copy for the big city papers had worn some grooves deeper than others. That one was pretty deep.

In contrast to the national press, the *Elgin Tribune* wasn't sensational at all. No longer did the broadcast and print media just follow the dictum, "If it bleeds, it leads." Now it had to bleed a lot. Hurt a lot. And create anxiety, shock whenever possible, and fear.

Always fear.

"There but for the grace of God" stories seemed to be the norm. Less sensational news was still reported, but those stories ended up on the back pages and the inside columns, lost among the celebrity gossip, ads, and obits. Read a paper, watch a newscast — you could only conclude that murder, rape, accidents, attacks, crimes, crashes, and calamities of every kind were not only common, they were *everywhere*. And they happened *all the time*. One national news commentator had taken to ending his broadcast with the admonition, "Remember, friends, keep your doors locked tonight." Most of the country did. In the face of such overwhelming evidence, how could they do otherwise?

Ernie did his best to resist. His was a small-town paper, his stories were small-town news. But on the rare occasions when we had a crime, particularly where some level of violence was involved, he succumbed. Big headline, front page, photo whenever possible. Auto accidents got their photo in color and bigger. If one guy punched another, it warranted a story. If one was white and the other brown — a headline. Blood spilled was always front-page news.

One day, right on the front page, was a photo of a woman we all knew, face a mess of bruises, crying baby in her arms. In the background, locked in cuffs and flanked by police officers was not her abusive husband or her drunken boyfriend — but her teenage son. In tears. Hands bloody from the wounds.

It was wrong. A private tragedy that had no business being shared. On some level, Ernie knew it.

"I've got an idea," he said to us one night over beers at Murphy's. "I'm not saying I'll do it . . . not sure it even makes sense, but what if I prioritized my stories by importance and not by impact?" The fact that such an idea could sound so revolutionary caught us all by surprise. It reflected how far things had slipped.

We knew he wanted to try, and we promised to give him plenty to write about. With the very next issue, the *Elgin Tribune* began to change. Stories that affected lots of people were right up front. Those that concerned only a few went to the back.

Sports, of course, still commanded a hallowed section all to itself — nobody ever expected that to change. But the local crime report — a guilty pleasure read by almost everyone? Ernie dropped it completely.

It was a three-car pile-up on the east edge of town that really tested him. The accident wasn't caused by drunk driving, and it wasn't caused by excessive speed. It was just bad luck, and one of the drivers died. Chuck, Matt, and Ritch, all members of Elgin's volunteer fire department, were there just after it happened. It was a bad one, as bad as they'd ever seen.

And Ernie was there, too.

He shot at least a roll of film.

When the paper came out two days later, there was no photo on the front page. There was no photo anywhere. And the story — only a few column inches, was on the back page.

Three months later, the Association of Small Western Newspapers, at their annual conference and symposium, gave Ernie Joiner and the *Elgin Tribune* the equivalent of the Pulitzer prize for journalistic integrity. The Tribune's new approach to news had itself become news. A few other small papers did the same — not many but a few. Ernie felt pretty good about that and about the welcome uptick in circulation that followed.

A new masthead for the *Elgin Tribune* was unveiled a few months later. The motto, "Lead Based on Need," made perfect sense.

We tried to thank him officially, as the city council, for improving the quality of life in our town. But Ernie would have none of it.

When I see him tonight, though, I mean to thank him for sure. And tonight, at least, I think he'll accept.

CHAPTER SEVENTEEN
EIGHT HOURS LEFT

NINE O'CLOCK NOW. Eight hours left. An eight-hour shift. An "easy eight," like the graveyard workers at the apple cannery in town used to say. Eight hours. Just eight hours.

How many breaths will I take in those eight hours? How many heartbeats, how many blinks? I can no longer tell if the time is passing slowly or quickly. I no longer care. All I know is that it IS passing — the last of it now, the very last of my allotted share. I can't stop the clock, and I can't turn it back. But at least I can remember.

At least I can do that.

The last year of our first term was a good one for the SOGs and for Elgin. That was the year that Leigh really hit his stride.

First it was medical marijuana. When the Feds raided one of Elgin's local medical pot farms, we were there the next day — the whole council planting illegal seeds to grow an illegal crop for the simple reason that sick people in pain depended on it. If anyone professed to be unclear on that concept, Leigh was more than glad to sit them down and explain it to them.

When the administration at Elgin High School started getting complaints about their Life Skills classes, particularly about the discussion of birth control and condoms, we took the problem off their hands. Free condom dispensers appeared around town. None of us admitted to knowing where they came from, but Leigh didn't care at all who saw him refilling them when supplies ran low.

Elgin was lucky enough to have a small family planning clinic in town back then, funded by a not-for-profit foundation that was forever running out of money. It just so happened that we were the clinic's landlords. The city actually owned the small building where it was located. All of us on the council were in favor of simply giving them the place — they never seemed quite able to pay both the rent *and* the city taxes in the same month. Without the rent expense, it seemed like they might be able to stay afloat. That was when staff informed us that gifts of public funds were not only frowned upon by many taxpayers, they were clearly against the law.

It was Leigh who came up with the idea of a "tax-exempt zone." Some cities had enterprise zones, others urban renewal zones. We created a tax-exempt zone. The fact that its boundaries exactly matched those of the family planning clinic? To the five of us on the council, that seemed perfectly reasonable.

Staffing for our low-income childcare center turned out to be a tougher problem. Leigh again. He hit upon the solution in an entirely unlooked-for quarter: Rhonda Gillespie, our town hooker.

Chief Reber did his best not to bust her, but there was a statute on the books, and an occasional complaint was called in. At such times, the chief had no choice but to give Rhonda a talking-to. He never arrested her — though as small as Elgin was, a visit from Chief Reber amounted to almost the same thing.

Everything eventually ends up in front of the city council in a small town — Rhonda was no exception. No, she wasn't there in person, and she was never mentioned by name, but in Elgin it's easy to "tell the players" without a scorecard. We had a debate about Rhonda at a public meeting. It was a damn good one.

Most cities pass ordinances to push their similar "problems" outside the city limits. The offending behaviors: homelessness, skateboarding, cruising hotrods on Friday nights, or the sort of cruising that Rhonda occasionally practiced.

Instead of ducking the issue, we tried to understand it.

Would a woman, if given a choice, take *any other job* than the one Rhonda occasionally chose? As a city council, we thought that was probably true — if not in a hundred out of a hundred cases, then at least in ninety-nine. It was Leigh who posed the follow-up question. Leigh, whose respect for women was the model that the rest of us SOGs tried to emulate.

"So, in the case of that woman, that one woman in a hundred, or more probably in a thousand or ten thousand. In the case of that particular woman who chooses that particular profession of her own free will, if she isn't doing any harm to herself or to others, do we have the right to say that her choice is wrong?"

We didn't much like the obvious answer. Leigh liked it least of all. But we could not deny it.

This wasn't an abstract question for us. We all knew Rhonda. So far as I'm aware, none of us knew her in that way, but we all knew her and liked her well enough. She wasn't a drunk. Sure, she scraped along on not very much money, but she wasn't a mess. She got lonely sometimes. She liked kids but didn't have any. She liked men but didn't have a steady one. We all agreed that we wanted to keep Rhonda from getting turned in again. It was an embarrassment for her — and Chief Reber had better things to do.

It was on our next trail run that Leigh proposed the solution.

Out behind the police station, we had a trailer intended for a low-income childcare center, an idea we all supported. But there wasn't enough money in the budget to pay for staff to run it and might never be.

Because Leigh came up with the scheme, we drafted him to approach Rhonda. Truth be told, none of the rest of us would have had the courage or even have known how to begin.

A few weeks later, the city council took two official though totally unrelated actions. At least they were unrelated on the agenda. They also went unreported — though Ernie Joiner was in attendance as usual.

The first was the establishment of a 7 a.m. to 4 p.m. low-income childcare center in the portable trailer out behind the police station. The second action established an adult wellness center — open from 8 p.m. to midnight by appointment only in that very same trailer — with the very same staff. Best of all, the fees collected from the latter operation would fund the former and provide the sole staff member with an acceptable living wage and full health benefits.

Regular medical check-ups and close proximity to the police station insured that there would be no trouble. To no one's surprise, certainly not Leigh's, Rhonda went on to get training in early childhood development, and she trained a second wellness counselor when she could no longer keep up with the evening trade.

CHAPTER EIGHTEEN
SEVEN HOURS LEFT

"MR. DAVIS, YOU have a visitor." Cervantes's voice is bringing me back, back from where I've gone wandering in those twilight woods toward that summer place, toward those lights in the trees. Back to this cell where the time hasn't stopped slipping away. Hasn't even slowed.

"Jesus, Ed . . . from where all this started in little old Elgin, how the hell did we end up here?" It's Joiner, which means that it is ten o'clock already. Probably the last ten o'clock I'll ever see.

In spite of what my official daily schedule says, there is to be no interview, and we both know it. Ernie has pulled some strings with some people. I don't know what strings, I don't know what people, nor do I ask. All I know is that I get to spend an hour with a friend. A friend who has watched and rooted for our home team from the beginning.

Ritch, Rory, and Mike took the lead on the council in 2008. We didn't plan it that way; it just happened.

Our budget, as always, was a mess. To make matters worse, the folks in Washington had decided to virtually eliminate what little money they were still doling out to local governments for social service programs. But they weren't abandoning the needy — no, far from it. Instead, they had simply decided that "faith based" charities were the most efficient way to address the needs of those less fortunate than themselves, which was almost everybody. At the instant our local safety-net funding was being yanked with one hand, Uncle Sam was extending his other hand to the churches, and it was loaded with cash.

Becoming a church was Ritch Foster's idea. "They may have walked all over the idea that God and government shouldn't mix, but having done that, they can't and won't challenge the sanctity and legitimacy of a church. Any church. How could they?"

After a sparsely attended council meeting adjourned late one night, and with no one but Joiner, Stedman, and Reber still in the audience to bear witness, the O

Be Joyful Church of Redemption and Hope came into existence. Five deacons were appointed — the city council members of Elgin, California. Pastor Stephen S. Stedman was chosen to serve as the spiritual advisor. It was mere coincidence that the stated goals of the church happened to reflect, exactly, every social service program that we on the council had been forced to cut.

It was no surprise that the story of the new church's creation and mission never made the pages of the *Elgin Tribune*. But Ernie did report — with much fanfare but few details — that Elgin's food bank and homeless shelter had found a new source of funding.

Mike took on recycling that year. He started with his classroom and worked out from there. His goal: to throw *nothing* away. He did the research, got the kids involved. Pretty soon it wasn't just his classroom, it was all of Dunbar School. The school district office took notice when they were informed, much to their surprise, that garbage pickup was no longer required at Dunbar. They also liked the newly mulched garden, and when harvest time came, they were glad to have the school serving its own vegetables in the cafeteria.

It wasn't long before we got the city sanitation staff on board. Changing the culture of garbage is no mean feat, but once sanitation got behind the concept, there was no stopping them. Their monthly customer statements started going out with encouragement to not purchase anything that couldn't be recycled. And they created a mission statement that was simplicity itself: "Don't throw anything away!" It was plastered on their letterhead, on the outside of their envelopes, and the sides of their garbage trucks.

But garbage, as anyone who has studied it can tell you, is really about money — and it was money that finally turned the trick. When sanitation instituted the "No Can, No Cash," program, things really started to change. As soon as customers understood that if they didn't put a can out for their weekly pickup, they wouldn't get *billed* for that pickup, the volume of garbage all over the city started to shrink. And it just kept shrinking. Sure, the paperwork was a nightmare and monthly billings decreased. But sanitation soon realized that the extra accounting expenses and reduced income were offset hundreds of times over by the savings from shortened garbage runs and reduced wear and tear on their equipment. Most significantly, the town landfill, previously thought to be near capacity, now looked like it would serve Elgin's needs into the foreseeable future.

And all over town, well mulched flower and vegetable gardens sprang up — more gardens than ever before.

With Rory, it was traffic. "We've got two choices," he said when yet another stop sign was proposed for yet another street where traffic had once flowed freely. "We can provide structure, or we can provide control. We've been trying control for years, and look where it's gotten us. There are so many stop signs in Elgin now that it takes twenty minutes just to drive across town — a trip that shouldn't take five. Adding more signs is just making it worse. I say let's get rid of all of them."

It sounded nuts at first — at *least nuts* and maybe really unsafe. But Rory stayed with it. He dug out the statistics with a little help from Chief Reber. Soon the picture became pretty clear. Most of our traffic tickets were issued at stop signs. Most of our traffic accidents happened at signed intersections. Our stop signs were looking more and more like accident magnets than a solution to traffic problems.

"There was a time not that long ago when we got along just fine with the one stoplight in the middle of town." Rory made his pitch to the council when he presented his findings. "We have not grown that much, and there aren't that many more cars. People have just forgotten the basic rules of the road. They've forgotten how to drive — because we've let them forget. We've tried providing control. Let's try providing structure instead. And maybe a few driving lessons."

In the face of great protests from the neighborhoods that had lobbied to put them in over the years, we pulled out most of the stop signs, even added a couple of roundabouts.

Damned if it didn't work.

In the beginning, it took a pretty aggressive enforcement campaign on the part of the chief and his men. But once people got the idea that the signs were gone in Elgin and the rules of the road applied to everyone, it worked surprisingly well. Once again, to Rory's great satisfaction, it was possible to drive across town in less than five minutes, without once honking your horn at a clogged intersection.

"You guys did alright." Ernie, when our time together is almost up. "We both know I'm really not here to do an interview, but is there anything you want to say? I promise it will get published, even if Trent's goons try to prevent it. Especially then."

I don't know how to answer him. This is the time, the moment when I'm supposed to make some pronouncement. To dig deep and come up with the words that will give all this meaning.

"Mostly, Ernie, I'm tired. Mostly it doesn't make any sense to me. Any of it. I don't want to die, I know that. I don't want to never see my kids again, never see Jan again. I don't want to never run again in the hills with the SOGs or go to a movie with Jan on a weeknight, just the two of us. Or see the sunset over Sonoma Mountain. That's all I know. It's all I've got. I'm sorry."

"You're the least sorry thing about this whole sorry mess. You know that, don't you? Before I'm done I'll make sure others know it too. A lot of others. I'm a newspaper man, remember. "Lead Based on Need." People need to know this story. The real story.

"You are a front page, top of the fold, banner headline in my book and in my paper, and you will be until I run out of ink and there's no more paper for printing.

"Thanks, Ernie."

"Thanks, nothing. What happens here is *not* going to be forgotten. I want you to remember that." He is almost ordering, then his command becomes a plea. "I need you to remember it."

"I'll remember, Ernie." Whether it is just for the remaining few hours or into some unknown beyond, it is what he needs to hear me say. And as I utter the words, I realize that I need it too.

Maybe memory is all there is when everything else is gone.

Maybe that has to be enough.

CHAPTER NINETEEN
SIX HOURS LEFT

THE HOURS ARE STARTING to go faster now, racing by. The long marches of the night aren't long at all. And the march is more like a sprint, a dash to the finish.

I know, as I hear the door open and Steve's footfalls in the hallway, I know that the last appeal has failed. I glance at Mr. Cervantes. He knows it too.

I've never seen Steve look so bad. So lost. Then it occurs to me — he is one of my oldest friends, probably the person I've know the longest. That means I'm probably the same for him.

He's not just here to tell me that the appeal failed, that the Supremes have as much as admitted that due process no longer exists in our country.

He's here to begin telling me goodbye.

"It's a bitch, Wedge." Not very proper language for my personal pastor, but Cervantes doesn't seem to notice. Or be listening. Steve looks at him a long moment before he goes on.

"You should see the crowds outside, more coming all the time. It's not a mob yet, but it could be. The Feds guessed wrong on this one. If things break loose, there are too many people out there for them to handle. This prison was designed to keep people in — not out." He is looking at Cervantes again. He hesitates, then leans in close.

"Give me the word, Wedge." He is whispering now. "Give me the word, and five minutes after I walk out this door a thousand people will come in here and get you."

"You can't be serious."

"I'm stone cold serious. They're out there. They're ready. You shouldn't go down like this." Now I see the tears in his eyes. "You can't go down like this."

"Steve, play it out." We're sitting, facing each other, head-to-head, arms draped around each other's shoulders. Now I've caught his tears. "I want it . . . God how I want it. But you've seen the guns on these walls. This isn't a prison anymore, it's a fortress. Maybe it would fall . . . I think maybe it would. But what about the cost?"

Cervantes makes a noise, on purpose I think. Yes, on purpose. Steve doesn't hear. I look up, and the guard's eyes are on mine. He shakes his head. Not a warning. More a request, an appeal.

"I can't do it, Steve."

"I know you can't. I knew before I asked. What do you want me to tell Jan?"

"To keep it from happening. To stop it if she can. The crowd will listen to her. Tell her to let them know that I don't want any more bloodshed. Tell her that the last, best thing they can do for me is not break in here. That just plays into Trent's hands. Tell her that."

"Anything else?"

"No. She knows already. She knows. Thank you, Alberto."

"It's been an honor, Wedgewood . . . right from the start. An honor."

And now he's gone. Even the echo of his footsteps in the hallway is gone. I will see him once more, but that will be different. He will be Pastor Stedman then. And he'll say words to me, read words to give me comfort and strength as we walk together.

He'll do his job.

He always has.

Chapter Twenty
Five Hours Left

THE SOGS GOT reelected for a second term. Turnout was high, opposition low, and the campaign, like the first one, was actually fun.

We kept at it, trying to make a difference anywhere we could in big ways and small.

It was the six-year-old who accidentally shot and killed his four-year-old brother — with a handgun the family had forgotten they even owned — that set me in motion. We were all devastated by the tragedy, the whole town, but I couldn't get it out of my head. I couldn't help but think that there was something we might have done to prevent it.

It was the "why" questions that were finally too much for me.

Why did we focus on the "accident?" Why did we think that the parents must be negligent? Why did we want to chalk it up to bad luck instead of asking the real question: why guns at all?

The question I couldn't get out of my head was why didn't we just get rid of them?

And so — with a lot of help from my running buddies, we did.

The proclamation we passed didn't have the force of law. The Second Amendment still held — had been elevated, in fact, to the level of a holy writ. But we were the City of Elgin, California in the year of 2010 — and within our town borders we decided to repeal it.

We started to collect the guns.

It was voluntary, of course. Almost ceremonial. The word got out. A disbelieving nation of gun owners — and an enraged administration under newly elected President Jonathan Trent — watched. And waited.

On a Saturday afternoon not six months ago, right on the steps of the city hall, we held a town festival like none Elgin, nor anywhere else, had ever seen. The "Freedom from Firearms Festival." Freedom for our town and freedom for ourselves. There were food vendors, balloons (not helium), banners, even a local band — Cynthia Carr and the Carrtunes — providing entertainment. Not everyone in town turned out, but plenty did.

For the first time since that little boy was killed by the forgotten handgun, the town started to feel good about itself again. I never owned a gun myself, so had no frame of reference. But one old man, who reluctantly tossed his bulky service revolver into the dumpster we'd provided, actually smiled when the weapon left his hands. "It was heavier than I thought," he said. "Heavy on the mind. I'm glad it's gone."

When Chief Reber stepped up to the dumpster, I felt obliged to join him there. He had a gun collection at home, we all knew that and guessed he'd probably keep it — unloaded and under lock and key as he always had. But the weapon he had with him that day was special.

"A Colt Peacemaker," he said, displaying it for the crowd and the GBS cameras that were recording it all. "Mayor Davis, this is the gun that won the West." I had rotated into the mayor's seat, and all the SOGs knew that this was my day. "I gladly present you with this relic of the past. I hope by its disposal we can make a better future for ourselves and our town. I now officially surrender my weapon."

He handed it over to me butt first as was only proper.

The pop must have been a balloon — a big one close at hand. Dave jerked, I jerked. A deafening explosion erupted. Between us. When the smoke cleared — and there was plenty of it from that cannon of a handgun that Dave had loaded years earlier and never discharged — Elgin's Police Chief, my good friend Dave Reber, lay on the steps, dead at my feet.

The GBS cameras had captured it all. Every awful second. For weeks, it was impossible to be near a television set without seeing it played again and again. The network finally stopped running it when they were certain it had served its purpose.

But the tape in my head has never stopped playing.

It's about to, though.

It is only a matter of time.

CHAPTER TWENTY-ONE
FOUR HOURS LEFT

THEY CALLED IT a "civilian tribunal." After Afghanistan and then Iraq, military tribunals had become almost commonplace.

They called me a "constituent combatant." It made me sound like a fighter, a soldier — which was exactly what they wanted.

There was no denying that I had killed a man. A friend, in fact. That it was obviously an accident didn't matter in the least.

I had committed my offense while depriving a citizen of his sacred right to own a gun. Killing Dave was secondary. Challenging President Trent, whose campaign platform included mandatory gun ownership for all citizens over eighteen — was the real crime.

I was done before I started.

Jury trials had already been subverted by Trent. The old selection procedure had proven far too time-consuming and subject to chance. Juries were now chosen by a qualified committee. State jury selection sped up the process — from the beginning to the almost always foregone conclusion.

The standards of evidence had changed as well. DNA proof was no longer allowed — it took the element of judgement out of the process. Yes, the element of fairness.

With TIA, Total Information Awareness, there was such a wealth of sensitive information available that it had to be screened before it could be released to defense counsel, screened by qualified government professionals. Screened in such a way that the discovery process simply ceased to exist. Cases could only be tried on the information the government deemed safe to release. Even if prosecutors didn't intend to use the screening to their advantage, it almost always worked out that way.

In any case, mine was not a jury trial. I went before a civilian tribunal: three judges specifically appointed and approved by the attorney general for this specific task, my specific case.

While the proceedings themselves were public and aired dawn to dusk on GBS, the deliberations were private. The verdict was never in any doubt. I had great legal counsel, the best. But they essentially had nothing to do, and we all knew it.

I was guilty as charged.

Three months after Dave Reber died on the city hall steps, the civilian tribunal convened. Three days later, I was convicted and sentenced to death. Three hours after that, I was driven the short distance up Highway 101 from the Federal Building, stripped of my clothing, my belongings, and my freedom — and deposited in this cell.

Right here.

And in just over three hours, I'll finally take my leave.

Chapter Twenty-Two
Three Hours Left

YEAGER IS HERE in my cell now, trying to collect his thoughts from the look of it.

In the hall, Cervantes is listening intently.

I am all ears.

"Mr. Davis. Here is what I have been instructed to offer you." His voice is steady. He has practiced this. "Your sentence will be commuted to life. Life, as you know, can be a very long time . . . " I think he is going off script here. I think this is him talking, not Trent. "A great many things can happen with the passage of time, pendulums that swing one way can swing back — they almost always swing back. What is considered a crime today may be viewed differently five years from now, ten years. I think it will be viewed differently." He is off script for sure — this is Yeager talking. More than talking, he is trying to convince me.

"You will be moved to a minimum-security facility. Not immediately, but eventually. You will be allowed to see your family once a month, perhaps more. In short, you will be allowed to have a life."

"And why would Trent do this?"

"I am only speculating, but I believe it's because he doesn't want your blood on his hands. He got too involved in this situation — publicly. I'm sure you know that there are thousands of people outside the gates of my prison right now. You may not know that there are tens of thousands more in cities across the country, standing outside in the dark, waiting. They know this thing has gotten out of hand. They know that their government has gotten out of hand. And if you die here tonight, they will know exactly who is responsible."

"What do I have to do?"

"Say you were wrong. That's all. Not about killing Chief Reber, of course — that was obviously an accident. You have to say you were wrong about the guns."

"If I say I was wrong about the guns, Trent wins, doesn't he? And none of it stops. Not the fear. Not the murder. Not the insanity. None if it."

"Perhaps — but you can't know for sure. And if you're dead, you'll never know."

The cell is silent. Absolutely silent. It seems that time has finally stopped.

"Thank you for bringing me this offer, the real offer." I hear my voice as I speak the words. I already know what I'm going to say next.

"What shall I tell President Trent?"

"Tell him to go fuck himself."

CHAPTER TWENTY-THREE
TWO HOURS LEFT

"YOU SHOULD HAVE said yes." Cervantes is standing just outside the bars of my cell.

"Maybe. I don't think so, but maybe. What's your first name, Mr. Cervantes?"

"Eliseo."

"Eliseo, what's on your mind? I'm about to spend the last two hours of my life with you. I've spent eight hours a day with you for most of the last three months, and I don't know anything about you. Now that I think of it, why are you still here? Wasn't Critchett supposed to come back on at midnight?"

"Yes, he was —but he won't. And you do know something about me. You know my family. My sister's name is Rosalba, and her little boy is Enrique. Enrique Pinola."

The little boy with the toy gun. The little boy that Chief Reber would have shot if he'd been carrying a real firearm.

"No accidents." I realize I'm mumbling to myself, still trying to make sense of it. "My wife is always telling me that there are no accidents. You being here can't be an accident."

"We don't have much time if we are going to do this."

"Do what?"

"Get you out of here

"What?"

"Warden Yeager was right — if you had ten years, you'd be free. I'm sure of it. You've got less than two hours. I'm not going to let you die."

"But the cameras?" He's at my cell door, opening it.

"Taken care of

"The guards?"

"Yes, there are guards." He escorts me out of the cell. We are moving down the hallway now.

"Mr. Cervantes — Eliseo —this is madness." We're at the end of the hall. The left end, at the door I came in three months ago. The door that stands between me and the rest of my life.

"I'm not going to let them kill you." I see his hand with the key as it moves towards the lock. I see my own hand reaching out to stop him.

"They will kill us both, you know they will." Our hands are on the door, frozen for an instant. "They will kill you."

He knows it's true.

His face tells me he has always known it. He is prepared to go anyway.

A stranger.

Ready to do this for me.

Because I once, unknowingly, did something for him.

CHAPTER TWENTY-FOUR
ONE HOUR LEFT

THE END NOW. Almost the end.

I would not have thought when this day began, that it could feel so good just to sit. So peaceful and good. Eliseo is in the cell, sitting next to me on the bunk. I think he's praying, saying words just under his breath, words that only he and his God can hear. It isn't a dialogue I can take part in. I know that now. But it is comforting to know that Eliseo can.

They will be coming soon. I'm not afraid yet — not like I thought I might be. There has been too much fear. Wherever I'm going, I won't be taking that fear with me.

And there's the door. The sound of the door. The sound of the footsteps. Some of the last sounds I will ever hear.

"Wedge, you should have seen her talk to them." He isn't Pastor Stedman yet. Not yet. He's just Steve, and he seems not to know that his face is awash in tears. "You should have seen all of them — your kids, the SOGs, all of them. It was a beautiful thing, Wedgewood. Beautiful."

"I'm so proud of them, Steve." I can hardly see for my own tears now. "So proud."

They have me on my feet. Yeager is in front of me, Eliseo on one side, Steve on the other. I don't remember standing up, but I'm on my feet. A guard I didn't see is putting chains around my ankles, and another is joining them to the chains that have appeared around my wrists. I know they're there but don't feel them, really. I don't feel anything.

The room, the Rust Room is just like I imagined. I don't know how we got here so quickly. Steve is reading now. He's got a hand on my shoulder, and he's reading. The words don't mean anything — nothing at all. But the sound of his voice is good. I am glad for his voice.

Now I'm at the post. That's what it is, a tall wooden post in the middle of the room with hooks to pull the chains through and straps to hold me up if I look like I'm going to fall. One of the guards reaches for the straps to tie me in place. Yeager shakes his head. I must look like I don't need them. I guess that's good.

As the guards step away, I get one look around the room. One last look. There are the cameras. Just cameras. There is the row of volunteers, their rifles still at their sides. I don't see them, really. I know they don't see me.

It is Stedman's face that I look on last. My old friend, Fat Albert. My old friend.

Then Yeager lowers the bag over my head, and the blackness begins.

Only it isn't blackness. Not entirely.

There is light. Faint light, twinkling as the wind blows the branches around. And I can see where the light is coming from now. The trees open up, and I can see. It's a lodge. A beautiful wooden lodge nestled in a forest glen.

And the doors are open to me . . .

And the light is streaming out . . .

And all my friends and family are inside.

Epilogue
Three Hours Later

ON THE MORNING of November 30, at 8 a.m, Eliseo Cervantes resigned his post as a death row guard at San Quentin Federal Penitentiary. Though it was clear that Ed Davis had died only a few hours earlier, the exact circumstances of his death were still unknown. The GBS cameras, broadcasting live from inside the prison, had cut off moments before the execution was to begin.

No official statement had yet been released.

No one knew why.

As Eliseo walked out the prison door for the last time, he saw a familiar face in the crowd, a face he'd seen just the night before. Ernie Joiner recognized him as well. It was Ernie who took down what Eliseo said, and printed it, word-for-word, in the *Elgin Tribune*.

"I don't know what he died of, but they didn't kill him. They thought he fainted; it happens sometimes.

They didn't have the straps on to hold him up. When they took the bag off to look at him, he was just dead. They tried to hide his face, but I saw it."

"Saw what?"

"Mr. Davis was smiling." Eliseo Cervantes blinked back tears, his own face still reflecting that last beatific expression, one he would never forget. "A good man died in that room, but they didn't kill him. There was no execution at San Quentin today."

The End